W9-AYS-848

SHELLY DUPREE'S
TO-DO LIST
(Formerly, in-debt diner owner,
now jackpot winner.)

1) Pay off mortgage on The Brimming Cup

2) Open a savings account

3) Get my hair done

4) Buy some quality makeup

5) Purchase a new wardrobe

6) Find myself a man!

Harlequin American Romance proudly launches
MILLIONAIRE, MONTANA, where twelve lucky souls
have won a multimillion-dollar jackpot.

Dear Reader,

Happy New Year! January is an exciting month here at Harlequin American Romance. It marks the beginning of a yearlong celebration of our 20th anniversary. Come indulge with us for twelve months of supersatisfying reads by your favorite authors and exciting newcomers, too!

Throughout 2003, we'll be bringing you some not-to-miss miniseries. This month, bestselling author Muriel Jensen inaugurates MILLIONAIRE, MONTANA, our newest in-line continuity, with *Jackpot Baby*. This exciting six-book series is set in a small Montana town whose residents win a forty-million-dollar lottery jackpot. But winning a fortune comes with a price and no one's life will ever be the same again.

Next, *Commander's Little Surprise*, the latest book in Mollie Molay's GROOMS IN UNIFORM series, is a must-read secret-baby and reunion romance with a strong hero you won't be able to resist. Victoria Chancellor premieres her new A ROYAL TWIST miniseries in which a runaway prince and his horse-wrangling look-alike switch places. Don't miss *The Prince's Cowboy Double*, the first book in this delightful duo. Finally, when a small Alaskan town desperately needs a doctor, there's only one man who can do the job, in *Under Alaskan Skies* by Carol Grace.

So come join in the celebrating and start your year off right—by reading all four Harlequin American Romance books!

Melissa Jeglinski
Associate Senior Editor
Harlequin American Romance

Jackpot Baby
MURIEL JENSEN

TORONTO • NEW YORK • LONDON
AMSTERDAM • PARIS • SYDNEY • HAMBURG
STOCKHOLM • ATHENS • TOKYO • MILAN • MADRID
PRAGUE • WARSAW • BUDAPEST • AUCKLAND

Special thanks and acknowledgment are given to
Muriel Jensen for her contribution to the
MILLIONAIRE, MONTANA series.

ISBN 0-373-16953-1

JACKPOT BABY

Visit us at www.eHarlequin.com

Printed in U.S.A.

ABOUT THE AUTHOR

Muriel Jensen and her husband, Ron, live in Astoria, Oregon, in an old foursquare Victorian at the mouth of the Columbia River. They share their home with a golden retriever/golden Labrador mix named Amber, and five cats who moved in with them without an invitation. (Muriel insists that a plate of Friskies and a bowl of water are *not* an invitation!)

They also have three children and their families in their lives—a veritable crowd of the most interesting people and children. They also have irreplaceable friends, wonderful neighbors and "a life they know they don't deserve, but love desperately anyway."

Books by Muriel Jensen

HARLEQUIN AMERICAN ROMANCE

MILLIONAIRE, MONTANA

MEET THE MAIN STREET MILLIONAIRES

Shelly Dupree—Owner of The Brimming Cup Coffee Shop

Sam & Ruby Cade—Army Officer (him), Mercantile Co-owner (her)

William Devlin—Owner of The Heartbreaker Saloon

Henry Faulkner—Retired Hardware Store Owner

Jack Hartman—Veterinarian

Finn Hollis—Retired Librarian

Dean Kenning—Barber

Honor Lassiter—Mercantile Co-owner

Kyle & Olivia Mason—Farmer (him), High School Teacher (her)

Nathan & Vickie Perkins—Doctor (him), Stay-At-Home Mom (her)

Sylvia Rutledge—Owner of The Crowning Glory Hair Salon

Gwendolyn Tanner—Boardinghouse Owner

Prologue

Shelly Dupree leaned her elbows on the old oak bar that ran the length of the Heartbreaker Saloon and wished she could consume enough alcohol to achieve the rosy glow some of the regular patrons were already sporting at five minutes to seven. But as a chef, she found taste too important to ignore when eating or drinking. And the bite and burn of Scotch or bourbon just didn't do it for her. She'd been toying with the same glass of gewürztraminer wine for an hour. Dev Devlin, owner of the saloon, stocked it just for her and served it with a flourish despite the teasing hoots and hollers of their friends.

She stared moodily at her reflection in the mirror hung behind the bar between two paintings of nudes, one reclining on lace, the other playing cards with a gentleman on her bed. Well, Shelly presumed he was a gentleman.

She refocused on her own face and thought she didn't look like a loser. Serious hazel eyes peered back at her, taking in short dark brown hair parted on the side, and an unexceptional but nicely symmetrical heart-shaped face. A pink turtleneck sweater, all that was visible above the bar, covered breasts that would never earn her a job at Hooters, but didn't require a push-up bra, either. She looked like an upwardly mobile young woman having a drink with her friends after a successful day at the office.

The truth, however, was that nothing in Jester, Montana, was upwardly mobile, particularly the merchants trying to make a living there. She was almost three months behind on her coffee-shop rent and was now on a cash basis with her suppliers of meat, produce and paper goods.

Several years of drought had decimated Jester, population 1,502, located on the eastern edge of the state near its border with North Dakota. To anyone passing through, the area was just a long expanse of rolling hills and dusty bluffs, and downtown Jester was but a two-block-long collection of charmingly antiquated buildings reminiscent of its pioneer history.

But to Shelly, Jester and its people were everything. She'd spent two years at the Culinary Institute of America in Chicago, and one year working as a sous-chef in the dining room of a Los Angeles hotel. But the other twenty-five years of her life had been spent in or around The Brimming Cup, a coffee shop her parents had owned and operated on Main Street since before she was born. It had become hers four years ago when her mother died of cancer, and her father followed six months later with a broken heart.

The people of Jester, who'd always been her friends, became her family. They continued to eat breakfast and lunch in the coffee shop, brought her the latest news, discussed world events with an enthusiasm unfettered by consideration for politics or political correctness, and simply made her want to stay.

She'd once had dreams of opening a fine-dining establishment in a big city, of imagining that the man of her dreams would walk in one day, fall madly in love with her and provide her with the sense of security and belonging that had died with her parents. She had work and her friends, but they went home to their families at night. She went home to Sean Connery, an old tabby tomcat who'd walked out of a snowbank last winter. When she'd opened the back door to offer him a saucer of milk, he had taken it as an invitation to move in.

Her parents had been loving but practical people, and they'd taught her that pipe dreams amounted to nothing and only hard work yielded positive results. So she stayed in Jester, knowing she'd miss home too much if she left. And there was no man out there for her, anyway. They were all married or looking for supermodels.

Unwilling to completely compromise her artistic approach to cooking, she'd added fine dining to The Brimming Cup's menu. But that had meant eliminating a few of the menu's standards and she'd gotten too many good-natured but serious complaints.

So she continued with the same fare her parents had

served for decades—burgers and fries, chili, stew, meat loaf, mac and cheese, sirloin steak, fried chicken, pie. Her life would go on as it always had.

But even pie hadn't been moving much lately. Skipping dessert had become an economy measure for many of her patrons. And while her lunch trade held steady, most of her regulars were eating breakfast at home to save money.

Still, business, though hardly brisk, had sustained the coffee shop until this winter. The snow had started in October and had hardly let up since. Now at the end of January, it had been a long four months without visitors, the Christmas trade had been disappointing thanks to the cautious national economy, and the town that had just gotten by was now in danger of slipping away altogether.

The Town Hall and the school were in disrepair, the church that all denominations shared needed a new roof, and the bronze statue of Catherine Peterson and her horse, Jester, for whom the town was named, was turning green. Everyone was mortified, but no one, particularly the town government, had the financial wherewithal to have it cleaned.

Now, in one hand, Shelly held the letter from the Billings attorney who managed her building, threatening her with eviction if she didn't pay the full two months she was behind in rent along with the current amount owing. She didn't have it, of course, and she was out of ideas on where to get it.

In her other hand was her list of lottery numbers.

Once a week she and eleven friends and members of the Jester Merchants' Association contributed a dollar and a list of numbers to a collective pot, and Dean Kenning, Jester's one and only barber and himself a contributor, drove to Pine Run to buy their ticket.

They'd done this every year for three years, and once they'd won forty-two dollars. They'd bought pizza, had a party and laughed about their big win.

She came to the Heartbreaker every Tuesday to watch the drawing on television. Her set at home was diseased and the picture unreliable.

She told herself philosophically as the time neared for the drawing, that no one could have everything in life. One was greedy to expect financial wealth when they were already rich in friends. But the fantasy of winning kept her going on particularly dark days. And this had been one of them.

Speaking of which, she'd hoped to pour out her troubles to Dev. They'd been friends since she'd taken over the coffee shop, and they served on the Downtown Christmas for Kids Committee of the Merchants' Association for the past three years. He had a reputation as a wild man, but he'd been a good friend and always had insightful and practical suggestions for dealing with her problems. He, however, was out.

Roy Gibson, who tended bar for Dev and was the spitting image of Willie Nelson, down to his gray braids, reached up to the television in a corner over the bar and turned up the volume.

"...lottery numbers of the Big Sky Country state of

Montana," the announcer was saying, "and her four-teen sister states in our Big Draw Lottery. This week's winning ticket is worth forty million dollars! Everybody ready?"

Shelly took another sip of her wine and studied the numbers she always played. Three, because there'd been three people in her family; eleven because that was the age she'd been when she discovered she really loved to cook; thirteen, because that was the sum of five and eight, her mother's birth month and day; seventeen, because ten and seven, was her father's October birth date; twenty-eight, because that was her age; and thirty-three, because that was her address on Main Street. Only the number that represented her age ever changed.

Dev always teased her that she'd be the kind of person whose computer codes or safe combination would be easy to crack because she used family dates.

"Ten," the announcer read as the camera closed in on a woman's well-groomed hand. It held a numbered ball that had been air-driven into a cup from a basket below. "Twelve! Twenty! Twenty-..."

Shelly lost interest at the absence of any of her numbers. There were eleven more sets of numbers besides her own on their communal ticket, but she knew these people. Their luck ran about as well as hers.

She may as well finish her wine and go home to Sean and a hot bath. She'd done all the prep work for tomorrow—tables were set, sugar containers and napkin holders filled, soup, stew and chili prepared. Five in the morning would be here before she knew it.

She paid Roy and was turning on the stool to step down to the hardwood floor when she heard the commotion outside. At first she thought it was just noisy teenagers driving by.

Then she heard the words ''We won!'' coming from beyond the saloon's swinging doors.

She stopped still on the stool to listen.

''We won! Dev, we won!'' It was Dean Kenning's voice.

She smiled to herself. Dev was part of the lottery pool. It sounded as though someone's numbers had earned them another pizza night.

Then she heard a woman's squeal, a man's uninhibited shout of excitement, then Dean's screaming laugh. ''We won! We won! We won!''

A little frisson of sensation ran under Shelly's breastbone as she leaped off the stool.

Patrons in the bar began to stream outside. Excitement was palpable and the little frisson under her breastbone was now beating like the wings of a hummingbird. Or maybe a condor.

The night was cold, snow drifting gently in the light of old turn-of-the-century streetlamps. Dean, in front of his barbershop at the end of the block, read a set of numbers to Dev, who stood under a light, unaware of the falling snow, checking them against the ticket.

He looked up, pale and clearly shaken. ''We *did* win,'' he whispered.

Ever a realist, Shelly pushed through the crowd to take the ticket from him. "Let me see that. Read them again, Dean. Slowly."

Dean, a big, ruddy-faced man who knew everyone and everything in Jester, read them again. People were pressing around her, looking over her shoulder, blocking her light. It had to be a trick of the shadows cast on the ticket.

She followed every number with her finger, heard Dean read every number on the sixth line of the ticket—the winning line. They were Gwen Tanner's numbers because she, like Shelly, had played her age—twenty-nine.

Shelly looked up at Dean, unable to speak. She parted her lips, but her throat refused to make a sound.

"How much did you win?" someone in the crowd asked.

"Forty—million—dollars!" Dean shouted, hands raised to heaven.

"That's…" Dev was calculating. "Three million, three hundred and thirty-three thousand, three hundred and…well, you know. One of those numbers with threes that go on forever!"

"There'll be taxes." That brutal dose of reality was provided by Wyla Thorne, a pig farmer twice divorced, who usually invested with their group but had grown tired of the disappointment. Her life, Shelly guessed, judging by the woman's attitude, had been full of it. Jack Hartman, the veterinarian, had bet in her place.

"We'll still be millionaires!" Dev said, grinning from ear to ear. Then he wrapped his arms around Amanda Bradley, Shelly's friend and Dev's nemesis. Amanda owned Ex Libris, a bookstore that shared the building that housed the Heartbreaker. She and Dev were at odds about everything. But he'd apparently forgotten that in the joy of the moment as he waltzed her out of earshot.

"Do you know what this means?" Dean asked, hugging Shelly, bringing her thoughts back to her own good fortune.

She nodded, afraid to speak the word aloud. "Solvency. Maybe even..." It was a word most merchants in Jester never even considered. "Wealth!" she whispered reverently.

He laughed and, putting an arm around her shoulders, raised the other in a roundup gesture. "Come on, everybody. I'm buying drinks!"

They partied at the Heartbreaker for hours and it was three in the morning before everyone finally went their separate ways with promises to meet at The Brimming Cup the following morning. They'd commissioned Dean to hire an attorney for their group, who would call the lottery commission in the morning and find out the procedure for claiming their winnings.

Shelly sat alone in her dark living room—thinking she'd never be able to sleep and she had to be up at five anyway—and dealt with a weird and out-of-place trepidation.

Things were going to change, she'd realized in alarm about an hour ago.

Twelve people whose businesses had been hanging by a thread had just won enough money, even after taxes, to support themselves through old age if they were careful and invested wisely.

She made a note to herself to find out what in the heck a Roth IRA was. Everyone was saying it was the thing to do with their money.

That was already a small suggestion of change. People who never thought beyond paying the rent or the mortgage were now throwing around financial terms she'd never heard before.

So her financial woes were over, but she couldn't help wonder just what had begun tonight. Life in Jester had been difficult, but predictable. Hot in the summer, cold in the winter, friends were family and family was everything.

The Merchants' Association of Pine Run, the county seat, had always laughed at Jester because nine businesses comprised the entire economic base of the town. Still, they'd managed to do their part in community and charitable events. Imagine, she thought, what they would be able to do now.

But would money affect the cohesive quality of their group? Would they build bigger houses and bow out of business life downtown, preferring lives of leisure? Or would some leave Jester altogether, finally able to chase their dreams?

She'd accepted that her life was here, but she'd

come to depend upon these people to give it its warmth and texture. They were what stood between her and loneliness. She didn't think of herself as a business or career woman; she thought of herself as a nurturer. She provided food that kept her friends going, she listened to their problems, told them hers, exchanged advice and affection.

She needed them!

"Okay, calm down," she told herself. "You tend to grasp and cling when you're frightened. Relax. Forty million dollars is a good thing."

Maybe it would bring her a man, she speculated, that little frisson of excitement tickling between her breasts again. She wouldn't want a man who was attracted to her money, of course, but wouldn't it be wonderful if her winnings made *her* more attractive?

What would it be like to have an unlimited wardrobe allowance? To have her hair done every week rather than every other month when she had it cut? To buy quality makeup instead of whatever was on sale at Cozy's Drugstore, and a fragrance that was advertised in *Vogue*?

Her excitement flared until she realized this was just another indication of the changes Jester was in for. Practical, hardworking Shelly Dupree was thinking about makeup…and men!

Chapter One

Shelly stood on the corner of Main Street, waiting for the light midafternoon traffic to pass, and stared at the check in her hand. One million, one hundred thousand dollars! The group had chosen the option of getting their money all at once rather than the annuitized $84,000 a year, and that had dropped the full figure by half. Still a fortune, as far as she was concerned.

She knew it was unsophisticated to revel in her good fortune, probably even reckless to hold the check in her hand for all the world to see, but she couldn't help it. She studied the neat, stick-straight ones printed on the check, then counted the zeroes. Five. Five zeroes! Seven figures! She was a millionaire!

"Hey, Shelly! You buying *us* lunch today?" Chet Brower waved from ten feet above her in the bucket of the city works department truck. He and his brother Chuck, who stood below in a hard hat, were changing the street signs in downtown Jester—a change insisted upon by Mayor Bobby Larson. Few of the merchants were in agreement—the old names went back to Jester history—but the whole town was terminal with lottery fever and the influx of new life it had brought to Jester, even before any of the Main Street Millionaires had deposited their checks.

Main Street was still Main Street, but the names of three major cross streets were being changed today. Her corner was now Big Draw Drive, a block east was Megabucks Boulevard and Lottery Lane was a block west. She'd expected things to change, but she hadn't been prepared for just how much.

News vans stood on every corner and seemed to spew an enormous number of people into downtown. They represented Billings, Helena, Missoula, even television stations from neighboring states. Reporters were scattered all over town, interviewing shop owners and people on the street, determined to make what they were calling the Main Street Millionaires national news.

Gawkers had arrived from Pine Run, from Baker, Billings, and even Helena. Everyone wanted a glimpse of the Lucky Dozen, another name their group had acquired.

Chuck came to Shelly and swept off his hard hat. The Brower twins were tall and big, the backbone of the city works department. They looked like linebackers, but thanks to their minister mother, they had hearts of gold.

"Marry me, Shelly," Chuck said, getting down on one knee on the sidewalk. "Then, buy me a Harley."

Shelly laughed and swatted his shoulder. Half a block away, a photographer drew a bead on them.

"Oh, let's see," she said, pretending to give it some thought. "That would make me the Bride of Chuckie, wouldn't it? Thanks, but I don't think so."

"No!" Still on his knee, he caught her hands. "Think of me as Charles! Prince Charles! You'd be a princess if you married me."

Shelly patted his thinning brown hair. "Then you'd have two princesses, Chuck. Because you're *already married.* You have three little redheaded children who look just like their mother. They'd be definite cogs in the works of a permanent relationship."

He held his hat to his chest and said with sober sincerity, "I could put up with it if you'll buy me a Harley."

"How about a burger?" Chet called from the bucket. "And you don't have to marry me."

Shelly looked up to see that Chet had taken down the old Peterson Drive sign with the bullet hole in it and put up the shiny new Big Draw Drive—white lettering on a forest-green background.

"Free lunch for all my regulars tomorrow," she said, a little stab of trepidation settling in her chest beside the tremors of excitement. "See you both?"

Chuck got to his feet. "You're a woman of style, Shelly," he said, sweeping his hat with a flourish as he bowed.

"Yeah, yeah," she teased, starting across the street.

"See you tomorrow." She blew Chet a kiss over her shoulder.

Harvey Brinkman's photographer shot her walking across the street while Harvey stood by, dressed as always in jeans and a flack jacket—a foreign correspondent wanna-be stuck at the *Pine Run Plain Talker*, circulation just over 6,000, because he had a reputation for erroneous reporting. And at just twenty-five, with a slight build, a pale complexion and curly blond hair, he talked like a gangster from the forties.

"Hi, doll!" he said as Shelly stepped onto the sidewalk. "Want to share with your fans what you're doing with the dough?"

"Nothing exciting," she replied politely. "Just taking it to the bank." What she really wanted to do was push him into the old trough in front of the Heartbreaker to clear his head and remind him that he was in Jester, Montana, not Afghanistan, and that this was the twenty-first century.

But the trough that once held water was now a planter, and if he hadn't figured out what time he was living in, there was little she could do to help him.

"There's got to be something you can tell us, Shelly," he pleaded, hurrying along with her as she passed the barbershop and headed for Jester Savings and Loan. "You selling the coffee shop and going to Europe? Staying home, but spending all your moola on new duds?" His cursory glance at her blue corduroy slacks and the wool-lined red parka that covered a blue turtleneck suggested that she really ought to consider that. "Nobody ever gets to see what you look like under that big apron you always wear."

She kept walking, determined to suggest at the next city council meeting that they put water back in the old trough.

Cameras flashed and microphones were pushed in front of her face as she walked through the savings and loan's leaded-glass double doors.

"Shelly! Are you finally going to live your dreams?"

"Can you tell us what they are?"

"What does the man in your life think of all this money!"

"Does it make up for not having children?"

She imagined her mother looking down on her and saying, "Patience, Shelly. Courtesy at all times. When you run a restaurant, your business is hospitality."

This wasn't her restaurant, but she'd been so conditioned to that creed that she tried to be kind to everyone and seldom lost her temper. Though this invasion of Jester was threatening to undermine her good humor. Still, she reminded herself, all these reporters, photographers and gawkers were eating regularly at The Brimming Cup.

She knew them by name now. When they were eating with her, they were friendly and fun and never asked questions, though they did make her feel as though she was being watched all the time. And when they were doing their jobs, they were unrelenting.

She answered their questions in order and smiled at

each of them in turn. "I love Jester, but I might travel a little, the only man in my life is Sean Connery, and I doubt that anything would ever make up for not having children."

"Sean Connery!" Gloria Russo from the *Helena Herald* gasped. She was short and plump and around Harvey's age.

Harvey leaned toward her as Shelly walked past them toward a teller. "Relax," he said. "It's a cat."

"Oh."

"Ladies and gentlemen!" Sidney Brown, manager of the bank, was tall, slender and gray-haired in a three-piece gray suit. He pushed the reporters back as they tried to follow Shelly. "How many times do I have to remind you that the business transacted in a bank is private? Please! You've been harassing my depositors all day. I'd call the sheriff on you if he wasn't already busy!"

Only slightly chastened, the reporters moved back to a refreshment table set up across the room with cookies and punch.

Shelly spent the next hour talking to Sidney about various savings plans, and opening a savings account until she could finally decide just what to do with her million. Her *million!* She loved thinking that word.

She deposited everything except four months' mortgage payments so that she could be one month ahead, a bonus for Dan Bertram, her cook, and several thousand dollars to "play with." The very thought gave her goose bumps. Money to play with. After the hardworking, frugal life her parents led, the words sounded like sacrilege.

When Shelly left the bank, the mayor and his assistant and self-appointed shadow, Paula Pratt, were on the sidewalk, being interviewed by the press. Bobby was wearing the earnest face he used in public.

He was in his late forties, a big, broad-shouldered man with light brown hair graying at the temples. He might have had a look of sophistication, except that he seemed always to be trying to project that and the effort seemed to negate the impression. Many of the townspeople considered him an opportunistic good old boy, but Shelly thought he was more complicated than that.

Randolph Larson, Bobby's father, had also been mayor twenty years earlier. He'd been a wildcatter with a nose for oil. Though the family had been wealthy, he'd been a humble man with a sense of family and civic duty. And he'd given Bobby everything he wanted.

Now Bobby, who'd played away his years at college and married a beautiful young girl who'd become a sour, childless, middle-aged woman always longing for Seattle society, was trying to fit into his father's shoes. But he was prideful rather than humble, and it was obvious to everyone, certainly even to him, that the shoes were just too big.

Consequently, hungry for the love and respect his father enjoyed, he took every opportunity for publicity, and fooled around on his wife, Regina.

Shelly suspected that, at the moment, he was doing it with Paula Pratt.

Paula was blond and shapely with a bra size higher than her IQ. She wore sheer blouses and lycra skirts and followed Bobby everywhere, calling him ''Robert.'' She carried a clipboard with her, and everyone speculated at Jester Merchants' Association meetings about what was on it. Some thought it was the cartoon section from the morning's *Plain Talker*. Other less trustful souls were sure she was taking down information to use against them later.

''...town's always been a wonderful place to live,'' Bobby was saying to Marina Andrews from the television station in Great Falls. ''And someday all the excitement will die down and it'll just be us again, but until then—'' he smiled with boyish charm for the camera ''—please come to Jester and spend your money.'' He laughed at his own clever patter.

As Shelly tried to sneak by them unnoticed, Bobby reached an arm out for her and drew her in front of the camera. ''And when you come, be sure to have pie at The Brimming Cup coffee shop owned by Shelly Dupree, here, one of our Main Street Millionaires. It's an experience you won't forget.''

''Okay.'' Marina made a throat-cutting gesture to her photographer. ''Got it. Thanks, Mr. Mayor.''

As Bobby and Paula moved on in search of another camera, Marina rolled her eyes at Shelly. ''Someone who *won't* stop talking on camera is almost as bad and someone who answers your questions with yes and no." She offered Shelly her hand. "I'm Marina Andrews with…"

Shelly nodded. "I recognized you. Isn't there something more important going on somewhere else in the world?"

Marina shrugged. "Well, there probably is, but this is the most interesting thing happening in Montana at the moment. I don't suppose you'd like to round out my interview by telling me what you think of Jester and how you think it'll be affected by twelve millionaires?"

"I think Jester's a wonderful place to live," Shelly replied, backing away. "And I think once all of you leave, it'll just be the same old Jester, and we'll be the same old people."

Marina looked her in the eye. "Now, you don't really believe that. You look different already."

Surprised, Shelly stopped where she stood. "But…we haven't met."

Marina nodded. "Yes, we have. I was here when that windstorm two years ago ripped the roof off your place and the movie theater and we could see right inside from our helicopter."

Shelly frowned. "I don't remember talking to you." Though she remembered that her photo had appeared in the paper. A friend in Great Falls had sent it to her.

"Well, you didn't. I got the story from the barber. You were busy trying to get tarps pulled over everything to protect it until the roofer could come from

Billings. It was a tough time for you, I know. And you didn't look defeated, but you looked resigned, as if your life would never be any different and you knew it.'' Marina shrugged her shoulders and smiled. ''But, you don't look that way today. You look…eager. Like maybe you could handle *some* things changing.''

''Some things,'' she agreed. ''Just not everything.''

''The right things.''

''Yes.''

Marina laughed with a journalist's cynicism. ''When you figure out a way to guarantee that, let me know.''

Marina's photographer pointed out Dean Kenning, closing up the barbershop, and they both hurried to waylay him.

Shelly went back to The Brimming Cup. She pushed her way inside and caught a whiff of the beef barley soup she'd made after the lunch rush was over and left on to simmer. It smelled wonderful. She'd read somewhere that many people associated the days of the week with a color—Monday was red, tough and trying. Tuesday was yellow, quieter but still a challenge. And so on.

But to her the days of the week were an aroma. Monday, garden vegetable; Tuesday, chicken noodle; Wednesday, beef barley; Thursday, ham and split pea; Friday, clam chowder.

She'd wiped off tables before she left, and apparently they hadn't been disturbed since. The chrome and blue vinyl of the tables and chairs in the middle of the room sparkled in the glaring winter sunlight. The blue vinyl booths up against the large plate-glass window with its blue-and-white-check valance were a slightly richer shade than the blue of the chairs. She'd been able to move the tables and chairs out of harm's way during the storm, but had had to replace the upholstery on the booths after tree branches and other debris ripped holes in the vinyl when the roof blew off.

She'd changed so few things in the shop since her parents had died that she sometimes walked in expecting to hear her father in the kitchen or her mother behind the counter, filling napkin holders or setting up. She looked around now, sensing something different, some disturbance of the familiar space.

She could hear Dan on the other side of the shelves that separated the counter from the kitchen. He'd put a Garth Brooks song on the jukebox as he always did when the place emptied and she walked toward the counter, humming.

That was when she caught sight of the baby carrier on the corner of the counter. It had been behind her line of vision when she walked in the door.

Something else for the lost-and-found closet, she thought, wondering how someone could have walked out without their carrier and not noticed.

"Dan!" she shouted, as she walked toward it. "Who left the baby carrier?"

There was a moment's silence, then his gruff voice came from the kitchen. "What carrier?" He came through the break in the shelving between the pie case and the coffee setup. He was tall and rough looking with a beaky nose and an attitude to match. He wore a paper hat, an apron over his kitchen whites and a scowl. He was a grump, but, like the Brower brothers, he was pure gold wrapped in a deceptive package. His wife had died ten years before, he'd raised a boy and a girl by himself, and now that they were in college in Texas, he worked as many hours as Shelly did. "There hasn't been a soul in here since you left."

"Maybe someone came in," she speculated, "took the baby out of the carrier, and when no one appeared to wait on them…"

Dan had turned toward the counter and interrupted her with a gasping, "Oh, God!"

"What?" she demanded, hurrying toward the carrier. She suspected what his widened eyes and horrified expression might mean but couldn't believe it.

"Maybe someone came in," he said, stopping in front of the carrier and staring, "and maybe they left when I didn't come out, but…but…"

"But, what?" Shelly leaned an elbow on the counter and looked into the front of the carrier. A fat-cheeked baby with bright blue eyes smiled gummily at her.

"But they didn't take the baby out," Dan said unnecessarily.

Chapter Two

"Oh, Dan!" Shelly exclaimed in a whisper. "Forgetting your baby carrier seems strange enough, but forgetting your baby?"

At her expression of indignation, the baby's smile crumpled and he began to cry. Both little arms went up in agitation and Dan reached for a piece of paper tied to the blue-and-white crocheted blanket with a diaper pin.

"Oh, no. No, baby. Don't cry." Shelly took a tiny hand in hers and shook it playfully as Dan opened the note. "It's okay. Don't get upset. I'm sure your mom will be right back."

Dan shifted his weight as he read. "Well, you're wrong about that," he said with a sigh. "Somebody left you this baby."

"What?"

The baby shrieked at her loud exclamation and Shelly pulled him out of the carrier, blanket and all, and held him to her chest where he screamed in her ear.

"'Please take care of Max,'" Dan read loudly over the baby's screams. "'I know you can give him all the love and money any little boy could need. Tell him I love him and I'm sorry.'"

"Sorry?" Shelly said in agitation. "Sorry? She leaves a helpless little baby in an empty coffee shop and she's *sorry?* You poor baby!" She held the screeching baby tightly to her and paced back and forth behind the counter, Dan staring at her in concern.

"Call the sheriff," he said. "He'll get a caseworker from Pine Run to come get him."

Shelly paced and shushed and talked nonsense, something she was surprised she knew how to do. Working with her parents in the coffee shop had left little time for the baby-sitting experience most other girls had acquired. But she found herself pressing her cheek to the baby's hot cheek and patting his back. She noted that the scent of roses clung to him.

"He's so small," she said as the sobs quieted somewhat.

Dan nodded. "Most babies are."

"How old do you think he is?"

He shrugged. "It's been so long since mine were that size. I'd say maybe six, seven months."

Even in her concern, Shelly was aware that there was something comfortable, *comforting* about the weight of the baby in her arms, about the little heart beating against her own.

She looked down into the unhappy little face, feeling a connection being made. Bright blue eyes looked back at her, a big tear perched on a bottom lid, stuck there. Max looked her over gravely then took a fistful of her hair. He studied it, then opened his mouth like a little bird and tried to bring the hair to it.

"Ouch. Ow." Shelly offered him her index finger instead. "Here, take this. It's used to being scraped and burned and otherwise abused."

Max took it, put sharp little gums to it, then leaned sideways against her with a little piglet sound of contentment.

An urgent, protective feeling raged through her, taking every nurturing inclination she'd ever had and squaring it to make her feel—oh, God—*maternal.*

For a moment she felt as though a pair of giant hands had shaken her, disturbed her whole being and her world, then set her down again. Absently she saw through the window that snow had begun to fall.

Great, she thought. Shelly Rose Dupree, millionairess, caught in a snow globe.

No! she thought fiercely. No, no, no! This was probably just some passing sensation every girl or woman experienced when she held a baby. But this baby wasn't hers. Someone had left it to her, but she was sure she'd change her mind in a heartbeat and be right back—probably before they even closed the coffee shop.

And she was not a candidate for motherhood. She loved children, sure, but she worked six long days a week, and she finally had some money to go places and do things. She couldn't take care of a baby.

Dan was right. She had to go see Luke McNeil, the sheriff.

There. The maternal feeling left as quickly as it had come. The past two weeks had been such an emotional roller coaster. She was just stressed. Not to mention shocked by having a baby left on the counter of her coffee shop.

"Okay." She tried to put Max back in the carrier, but he began to scream again, so she held him in her arms instead. "I'm going to see Luke. I hope he's in his office, and not out on a call. Can you close up for me? Put the soup in the fridge? I'll come in early and prep in the morning."

"Sure." Dan helped her into her coat, then took the gray sweater she kept in the back and wrapped it also around the baby. "Are you going to be okay? You need me to come?"

"I'll be fine," she said. "You take care of things here. Oh." She pointed to the purse she'd left on the table in the first booth when she came in. "Take that envelope sticking out with your name on it, and put the purse on my shoulder."

He did as she asked, then studied the envelope as he walked her to the door. "What's this?"

"Open it when you get home," she directed, then walked out into the snow, wrapping her coat around the baby. The sheriff's office was kitty-corner from The Brimming Cup.

As she waited to cross the street, Shelly became aware that Luke was not out on a call, but he did seem to be having some kind of problem. She could see his tall, strong, uniformed body in the middle of a throng of people holding placards. They were marching around him and shouting.

No News Is Good News! she noticed one of the signs read as the sudden disappearance of traffic allowed her to cross diagonally. Other signs read, Clear Out Of Jester! Go Bother Somebody Else! Money Talks. It Says, Get Out Of Jester! Dean Kenning was carrying that one, but he was smiling. She had a feeling he'd joined the crowd out of amusement rather than any serious disapproval of the presence of the news media.

Shelly pushed her way through the crowd to approach Luke. He was tall and dark and had Native American ancestors. "Can I talk to you for a minute?" she asked.

"If you're going to complain about the press," he said with a long-suffering sigh, "it's been taken care of. And then some."

"I wasn't," she assured him.

He looked surprised. "But you hate them."

"Yes, but I also realize we're news and that pretty soon we won't be and they'll all go away. Luke, can we talk?"

"Sure." He caught her arm and, opening his office door, pushed her gently inside. Then he turned to the protestors and said firmly, "You keep your voices down and stay out of the street."

Several nodded and everyone kept marching.

Luke closed the door behind him. He had a small, cluttered office, but in the past six years that he'd occupied it, he'd solved Jester's problem of nighttime vandalism, and two years ago he had caught a pair of prisoners who'd escaped from Folsom and were considered armed and dangerous. He had a toughness appropriate to his position, but he was a very nice man. At the moment, however, he was understandably preoccupied with the marchers and she needed him to focus on finding a solution to this baby.

He stopped in the middle of the office and turned to her. "What is it?"

She shifted her weight impatiently. "Luke!" She pointed to Max. "Have you completely failed to notice that I have a baby in my arms?"

He frowned at that, apparently unsure of her point. "I noticed. Whose is it?"

"I don't know!" she snapped at him. "Someone left him in the coffee shop. Can you check if someone's reported a baby missing?"

"No babies missing. What do you mean someone left it? How do you leave a baby?"

"They just did. I went to the bank to deposit my check and when I came back…" She handed him the note. "I can't have a baby. You have to call whoever in Pine Run takes care of abandoned children."

Max squirmed and fussed and she moved him into her left arm, hoping to placate him.

"You're not making sense," he said. "If you knew

someone left this note with him, why did you ask if there were babies missing?''

''I don't know. Just desperate. I thought maybe someone stole him, then decided they didn't want him after all.''

He considered that, then nodded as though that might be possible. ''I'll check again. Meanwhile—'' he put his fingertips to the baby's cheek ''—he feels hot.''

''Oh, no.'' She'd noticed that earlier, but it hadn't registered as a problem. ''Do you think he's sick?''

He shook his head. ''I don't have much firsthand experience with babies, except for having delivered a few. Why don't you take him to the medical center and have the doc check him out, and I'll see if I can round up somebody from Child and Family Services.''

''Good idea.'' As Luke picked up the phone, Shelly went outside again, sheltering the now-screaming baby against her body. The protestors parted ranks to let her through and she hurried across the street, down the block and around the corner.

Nathan Perkins was the quintessential family doctor. He was a loving husband, devoted father of three, and a friend as well as physician to most patients he saw. He deserved the respect everyone in Jester gave him.

But Nathan wasn't there, according to the young redheaded receptionist, who led her to a small examining room. Standing in for him was a tall, slender man with rich brown hair and a pair of gold-green cat's eyes that put her on the edge the moment she looked into them. They looked her over, went to the screaming baby in her arms, then back to her eyes with a disapproval that confused her.

But she didn't have time to think about it. She held Max out to the doctor. "Please," she said. "Is something wrong with him?"

He took the baby, his large hands covering the baby's torso. He walked around with him, putting a hand to his forehead and his cheek.

"Has he had his DPT shots?" he asked.

"Ah...?"

"Diphtheria, tetanus, pertussis vaccine," he explained.

"I don't know," she replied.

"His HI?"

"Um...?"

"Hemophilus influenzae B."

"I don't know. I run The Brimming Cup and he was..."

"When did this start?" he interrupted.

"I just noticed it in the sheriff's office when..."

Those eyes looked into hers again and stopped her cold. "Did you try baby aspirin?"

"No, I..."

"Cool bath?" He'd taken out a stethoscope and was listening to Max's heart while the baby latched on to the instrument.

"No, I told you I was in the sheriff's..."

He held a finger up for quiet as he listened. Then

he removed the stethoscope, put it out of the baby's reach, and asked with another direct glance into her eyes that had an angry quality to it she didn't understand, "Do you know what he weighs?"

"No, I don't. I…"

He leaned a hip on the examining table and held the baby to him, stroking his back and shushing him. He pointed her to the room's only chair.

She sat, her mind a whirl of the afternoon's shocking events and the doctor's inexplicably aggressive behavior.

"This baby is supposed to be your first priority," he said in a voice that had gentled only slightly and sounded as though it intended to preach. She suddenly realized what he must be thinking.

"Doctor, I'm…"

"How can you *not* know whether or not your baby's been immunized?" he interrupted again. "How can you not know what he weighs? How can you have a baby and pursue a lifestyle that lands you in the sheriff's office?"

She sprang to her feet again, tired of his accusations, whatever he thought.

"Because I'm not his mother!" she shouted at him. "He was abandoned in my restaurant by someone who left a note, saying she knew I could take care of him because I'm one of the winners of the lottery!"

He had the grace to look surprised, though not particularly apologetic. So she went on.

"And I was in the sheriff's office because going to

the authorities seemed to be the thing to do when you find an abandoned baby. What would you have done? Simply shouted at the baby like you shout at your patients?''

EVEN CONNOR COULD AGREE that he had that coming. He should have asked before he took on an accusatory approach to her parenting. But he'd seen so much child neglect and abuse in Los Angeles, where he came from, that he'd become a warrior in defense of children. And sometimes that meant getting mean with parents.

"No," he replied with a half smile. "I never yell at babies. I'm sorry. I mistook you for one of those women for whom the fuzzy glow of motherhood had worn off. When you couldn't answer any of my questions, I thought you'd lost interest in your baby.''

That honest admission seemed to defuse her anger, but only a little. She blinked wide, darkly lashed hazel eyes at him. "Well, maybe you should have asked.''

He nodded. "Maybe I should have.''

That might have defused her anger a little more, but he could see in her eyes that she resisted forgiving him. He'd hurt her feelings after all. She was another touchy hybrid like Lisa had been. She angled her chin, short, straight, glossy brown hair catching the light.

"Can you tell me what's wrong with him?" the woman asked, folding her arms, apparently determined to keep him at a cool distance.

That was fine with him.

"Actually, I think he's just teething," he said, putting his index finger into the baby's mouth. The baby sucked on it like a little vacuum. "You can feel the two central incisors just about to pop through. Here. Feel."

She gave him a disdainful look, then came closer and put her finger in the baby's mouth. "Oh." She smiled at the baby. "You're getting teeth, Max."

The baby laughed at her.

In all his years of internship, residency and practice, Connor had yet to see an ugly baby, but this little guy had a winning way as well as pink cheeks and bright blue eyes.

"I can't imagine anyone being able to just leave him and walk away," she said, her disapproval finally aimed away from him and toward the baby's mother.

"I know." He handed the baby back to her. "But I worked at an inner-city hospital in L.A. and I saw it all the time. And as incredible as it is, it's a better choice for the child than those who keep their babies then can't deal with them. You might give him a cold, wet washcloth to chew on, or freeze a bagel he can gnaw on. Just make sure he doesn't get a piece off and choke on it. Over-the-counter teething solutions help a little, too."

She held the baby to her and wrapped him up. "I can't have a baby," she said a little defensively. "I'd love to have one, but I work all the time." She looked at him as though she expected censure.

Instead, he nodded. "Some lifestyles just don't allow it."

"It's not a lifestyle choice," she said, her defensive tone a little edgier. "I mean, I'm going to have money now. I wouldn't have to keep the coffee shop, but it was my parents', you know, and I grew up in it. I watched them pour their hearts into it. I can't just sell it and move on."

He didn't know why she seemed to need his agreement, but she did.

"I understand," he said.

Apparently she didn't think he could. "I've never heard of you," she said, rocking the baby as he began to fuss. The words suggested that was his problem rather than hers. "Do you live here, or are you just helping out?"

"I went to medical school with Nathan," he replied, opening the examining-room door for her. "I visited last summer, and he told me if I wanted to come back, he'd give me a job. I liked it here, so I took him up on it. This is my third day as a resident of Jester."

"Well…learn to soft-pedal that aggression," she said, stepping out into the hallway. "Most of the people here are kind and neighborly and good to their children."

She offered the advice seriously. He took it humbly, eager to send her on her way so that he could put in his last hour here, get something to eat and go to his bed—such as it was. He'd been sleeping on a cot in the storage room upstairs until he found a place to live.

"Hey, Doc. How're you liking Jester?" Luke McNeil stood in the waiting room, hat in hand, chatting with Carlie Goodwin, the receptionist. She went back to work when Connor claimed Luke's attention.

Connor had been on call the night before, and the sheriff had brought him a teenager he'd picked up for drunk driving. The kid had cut himself on broken glass in a fall while trying to escape. Connor had liked McNeil and his caring but no-nonsense approach to law enforcement.

Connor went forward to shake hands with him. "I'm doing fine, Sheriff. Too bad about this little guy."

McNeil looked alarmed. "Is he sick?"

"No," Connor assured him. "I meant, it's too bad somebody abandoned him and left him to the mercies of the system."

"Yeah, well, the system's not working too well at the moment." He frowned in concern. "Every time the wind picks up around here, the phone lines go down. We have virtually no cell phone reception. I can't get through to Pine Run to get a caseworker here." He turned a subtly pleading look on Shelly.

She began to fidget. "I can't, Luke. I've never taken care of a baby. I wouldn't know what to do. A couple of hours would be one thing, but through the night? I...I..."

As though on cue, the baby grabbed a fistful of her

hair, yawned mightily, blinked deeply several times, then fell asleep on her shoulder.

Connor had never seen a woman look so terrified at the prospect of caring for a baby. What he'd taken for lack of enthusiasm about her baby when he'd thought she was his mother was apparently just inexperience. Or possibly simple unwillingness to deal with babies.

He couldn't help the animosity that stirred inside him. He knew it was indicative of his own personal dichotomy where babies were concerned. While he truly felt that people who didn't want children shouldn't have them, *he* wanted them. Yet the only women who seemed to cross his path were those who didn't. One of the many irreconcilable differences that had ended his marriage to Lisa a year ago was their divergent opinions on whether or not to have children.

This woman was certainly entitled to do what she wanted with her own life, but he wanted her to come to the rescue of this baby—at least for tonight. He couldn't keep it. He was sleeping on a cot in an upstairs room that had nothing else in it but supplies. And as long as Nathan was gone, he could be called out at any time of the night.

McNeil sighed. "Then, I guess we'll have to leave the baby with Connor, Shelly."

"With who?" she asked.

McNeil looked from her to him. "You mean you haven't even introduced yourselves?"

"No," she said. "He was too busy accusing me of child neglect."

Connor kept quiet. It didn't look as though there was any way he was going to be able to defend himself in this.

McNeil pointed to Connor. "Shelly, this is Connor O'Rourke, Jester's new pediatrician. Doc, this is Shelly Dupree, owner of The Brimming Cup and usually a very nice lady." He fixed Shelly with a serious expression. "Now, come on. You got to help me find a solution here."

Shelly rocked the baby from side to side, her mouth set in a pugnacious line. "We can't leave Max with him. He has a bad disposition."

McNeil studied her in puzzlement. "Now, I know that isn't true, Shelly, because I woke him up in the middle of the night last night with an injured kid and he was very kind to the boy. And he didn't yell at me, either."

"You wear a gun, Luke," she pointed out. "Nobody yells at you."

McNeil took each of them by an arm and led them to the old brown vinyl sofa and chairs. "I have a thought," he said. "Let's talk this through." He sat them side by side on the sofa, then pulled up a chair facing them.

He pointed to Shelly. "You're unsure of how to take care of the baby."

"Yes," she agreed.

"And you—" he indicated Connor "—are sleeping on a cot in the supply room."

"Yeah."

"So what if—" he smiled winningly at Shelly "—the doc stays the night at your place so that if you have a problem with the baby, he'll be there to help."

Her eyes widened. She looked at Connor as though he carried the Ebola virus.

"I'll try to get through to Pine Run tomorrow. I'll even drive down there, if I have to. But I can't do that tonight because I still have a crowd of picketers in front of the office and a bunch of reporters who've taken offense at their attitude. Come on, Shell. Give me a break. The other day when I was having lunch at your place, you told me you'd thought about taking in a boarder."

She didn't want to do this. It had trouble written all over it. In bold caps.

But the weight of the warm baby on her shoulder was scrambling her determination to have nothing more to do with him. She finally had life the way she wanted it. She was solvent. She could do things. She didn't know what yet, but when the opportunity arose, she wanted to be ready.

She couldn't afford to be sidetracked.

But this was just for one night. And it involved the grumpy doctor, but she could live with that if it would help Max.

"What do you think, Doc?" Luke asked.

Connor O'Rourke turned to Shelly, a look of clear

reluctance on his face. "You promise not to make my life miserable while I'm there?" he asked.

There was amusement in his eyes, but not a hint of a smile on his face. She wasn't sure if he was teasing her or not.

"If you promise not to make assumptions about me," she retorted stiffly.

"All right!" Luke said with relief. "Now we're talking." He stood, apparently anxious to get away before one of them had a change of heart. "I'll try to contact Pine Run first thing in the morning, and I'll see what I can do about tracking down his mother. Thanks, Shelly. Thank you, Doc."

"Yeah."

"Sure."

The door closed with a bang behind Luke, and the baby raised his head with a whimper.

"It's okay, it's okay," Shelly crooned, patting his back and rocking him. He put his head down immediately and went back to sleep.

"I live on Orchard Street," Shelly said, putting her purse on her shoulder and moving carefully to her feet with the baby. O'Rourke made a move to help her, but she glared at him and he took a step back. "On the corner of Peterson." Then remembering the street names had been changed this morning, she corrected herself with a sigh. "I mean Big Draw Drive. It's a yellow house with white trim and a Beware of Cat sign on the door."

"Should I be worried?" he asked with a very small smile. "Or is it a joke?"

"It's never been tested," she replied, shifting the baby in her arms. It was amazing, she was beginning to realize, how so small a bundle could feel so heavy after a while. Her purse fell off her shoulder with the movement and O'Rourke reached casually out to put it back. It was just a brush of touch through the thickness of her parka, but she felt it. She thought that odd. "I saved the cat from a snowstorm, so he's very devoted to me. If you were to shout at me, he might very well attack you."

He lowered his voice as he walked her to the door. "I'm martial arts trained," he said, and pulled the door open. "Is there anything you want me to pick up on the way home?"

She was surprised by the thoughtfulness of the question, considering the way he'd treated her in the beginning—and the way she'd treated him in return.

"I meant diapers, wipes, powder," he said.

She hadn't thought of that. And she couldn't see herself shopping with the baby in one arm and pushing a cart with her other hand. Experienced mothers had a way of doing that, she was sure, but she couldn't see herself managing it.

He seemed to be reading her mind. Or he simply considered her completely incompetent.

He pulled her back into the office and closed the door. "Hold on a minute. I'll get you a few diapers to keep you going until I can pick some up for you."

He took off at a lope and disappeared into a hall-way. He was back in a moment with a black soft-sided briefcase into which he'd placed several disposable diapers, a sample tube of antibacterial ointment and a sample pack of wipes.

"Whose briefcase?" she asked as he put it on the same shoulder as her purse.

"Mine," he replied, opening the door again. "We don't have anything as civilized as a paper bag, and you do have your hands full."

Again his consideration confused her.

His stomach growled and he grinned, putting a hand to it. "Sorry. With Nathan gone, I didn't have time for lunch today."

She was going to hate herself for this, but she said politely, "I make a good shepherd's pie, if you'd like to join me for dinner."

Surprise registered in his eyes. "I would, thank you." He pulled up the sweater she had wrapped around the blanketed baby and placed it so that it covered Max's head.

She hurried down the steps, moving carefully where the snow had made them slick. It was only a block and a half to her home, but she went to the coffee shop first to pick up the baby carrier. She tried to put Max in it to simplify the walk home, but he awoke and began to cry. She put her purse and the briefcase over her shoulder, threaded her arm through the handle of the carrier and headed home with the baby in her free arm, fast asleep again.

She tried to pick up the pace, but the complicated burden she carried forced her to slow down. She noticed the snow drifting over and around them in silent strokes. Snow was so much a part of winter life here that it was just another fixture of downtown, like the lights and the trees they'd planted in better times.

Dusk had fallen and the streetlights were on. Downtown was a little fantasy world, every shop outlined in white outdoor lights. The merchants had gotten together to trim their businesses for Christmas two years ago, and everyone had liked it so much, they'd left them up. The relatively small amount it had upped their power bills was a small price to pay for casting a glow in the middle of a cold, dark winter.

She hurried up the six steps to her cottage, smiling when her new sensor porch light went on. She fitted her key in the lock, reached in to flip on the living room light, then closed the door quietly behind her, the baby still asleep.

The cottage looked very different than it had when her mother had decorated it. She'd loved Victorian-style furnishings and had had the place cluttered with medallion-back sofas, chairs with doilies on the arms and spindly little tables covered with knickknacks. Shelly had sold everything but a little desk she'd put up in her bedroom and decorated in a plainer, more comfortable style. She had a red-and-cream-check sofa, a big beige chair by the brick fireplace, two wicker rockers she'd painted Chinese red with cushions she'd covered in yellow-and-green-flowered fabric.

There'd been a dining room right off the living room, but she'd taken out the table and chairs, since she never got to use them, and extended the living area into one great room.

The kitchen woodwork, which had been the same shade of blue as the restaurant, was now a mossy green color. She'd painted the walls a soft pink and pulled the colors together with a border of potted flowers in yellow and pink. A little square table that could seat four but was really more comfortable for two sat near a window that looked out onto her large backyard and the rolling hills beyond.

She always loved coming home. The restaurant was her life, because it had been her parents' life, but as a child she'd always been eager to come home after going to the restaurant after school. As an adult, she'd taken even more pleasure in her home. Though she spent precious little time here, it was a haven. A lonely haven, but still a haven.

She put the carrier on the table and placed Max in it while she put the other things down and removed her coat. He woke up instantly and began to cry. The cry turned quickly to a screech of displeasure. She changed him and tried to feed him, but he was too busy screaming.

"Okay, okay," she placated, picking him up again. "We'll just have to cook with one arm."

She learned, over the next hour, that that was not as easy as it sounded.

Chapter Three

Armed with a box of diapers and a bag filled with a few other purchases appropriate to the care of a baby, Connor knocked on Shelly's front door. He heard the baby screaming somewhere in the back of the house and wondered how Shelly was faring. The sound suggested she wasn't doing well, but he knew that sometimes there was just no way to stop the screaming. It had to go on until the baby exhausted himself.

And Max probably knew on some level that his mother had abandoned him. He had every right to scream.

Connor rang the doorbell and, when there was still no answer, tried the doorknob. It gave and the door opened, admitting him to a room that was cold and dark. He caught a glimpse of fat, upholstered furniture and a brick fireplace.

"Hello?" he called.

The only answer was "Meow?"

He peered through the shadows and spotted a pair of bright yellow eyes in an indistinguishable form perched on the back of the sofa. That's right. Shelly had talked about her cat.

He stroked the cat's thick fur, trying to remember his name. Mel Gibson? John Travolta? Sean Connery!

"Hey, Sean," he said, scratching between the cat's ears. "Where's Moneypenny?"

He saw a light toward the back of the house and followed it. He heard Sean leap down, then felt him race past his ankles into the kitchen.

Connor found Shelly standing over the sink, the baby propped on her shoulder, screaming, while she held his pudgy little legs to her with one arm and tried to peel a potato. It didn't appear to be going well. The three potatoes on the counter beside her still wore their peels.

Sean went to a food bowl in a corner of the kitchen and settled down to eat.

"Hi!" Connor shouted from the doorway to the kitchen.

She turned, the baby clutched to her with the hand holding the peeler. Her sleek hair was slightly disheveled and she looked frazzled.

"Hi," she replied with a sigh. "I know you're starving, but dinner's not going together very quickly."

He put the box and bag down on the floor, pulled off his coat and dropped it on top of them.

"Maybe it'll help if I take the baby," he said, walking toward her.

She aimed a hip at him to pass Max over and they

were eye to eye for the space of a heartbeat. He felt his heart punch against his ribs.

Cool it, Romeo, he told himself. *This is the wrong direction for you. So the blue turtleneck makes her hazel eyes an interesting shade of teal. So she looks tousled and vulnerable. This isn't the real her. She has a sharp tongue and she doesn't want babies in her life. You just freed yourself from a woman like that.*

"I noticed a fireplace," he said, settling the baby on his hip and pointing toward the living room. Max, surprised by the sudden movement, stopped crying. "Do you want a fire in it?"

"That'd be nice," she replied, leaning back against the sink as though handing him the baby had been a great relief. "I was so preoccupied with the baby, I just now remembered to turn up the furnace. Max won't let you put him down to build the fire, though."

"That's okay. I can do most of it one-handed."

"Then you're more talented than I am."

"Not necessarily." She looked like a woman who needed encouragement. "Potato peeling is definitely a two-handed job."

She accepted that concession with a smile. "Dinner will be about another hour. Do you need something to nibble on in the meantime?"

That sounded hopeful. "Do you have something?"

She went to the refrigerator and pulled out a small plate of hors d'oeuvres—water chestnuts wrapped in bacon, little puffy things he couldn't identify, and two slices of what looked like pepper jack cheese.

Maybe he'd fallen into something really good here.

"Do you always prepare hors d'oeuvres with dinner?" he asked as he accepted the plate gratefully.

She smiled. She had pretty white teeth and a small dimple in the left corner of her mouth. It snagged his attention.

"No," she replied. "They're left over from a party the Main Street Millionaires had last night to celebrate picking up our checks. Eat up. But let me get you crackers to go with the cheese."

She reached overhead to a cupboard handle and pulled. Nothing happened. Then she smacked the door with the side of her fist just under the handle and it popped open.

"House is settling, or something," she grumbled while removing several crackers from the box and adding them to his plate. "Want a glass of wine to go with that?"

He was already a little intoxicated with her closeness, but he replied, "Sure."

"Let me get these potatoes peeled, and I'll bring it to you."

He went to the living room, holding the plate out of the interested baby's reach. He found the light switch by the front door, then put the plate down on a low table. The baby's eyes followed his movements as he took one of the bacon-wrapped chestnuts to keep himself going.

"This'll give you heartburn," he told Max as he reached into a brass wood box and dropped two chunks of wood and a wad of newspaper onto the hearth. He sat down cross-legged beside them, pushed back a simple wire-mesh screen and, while holding Max on his thigh, stacked the wood.

He tore the newspaper into single page widths, then folded and twisted them into a sort of kindling. He pulled a page away from Max as he tried to draw it into his mouth.

"That's not what they mean by digesting the news," he said into the baby's scream of indignation. "I know, I know. You have big plans and someone's always changing them for you. Well, relax. I brought you some strained squash. Yum."

Connor spotted fireplace matches in a decorated tin cup on the mantel. He stood with Max, sat him on the beige chair right beside the fireplace, and while the baby screamed a protest at his abandonment, Connor lit the tinder, waited to see how well the draft would take, then added a third piece of wood at an angle atop the other two.

He straightened to see Shelly standing behind him with a glass of wine.

"Perfect fire," she observed as it caught the top length of wood. She handed him the wine. "Boy Scout or pyromaniac?"

"Thank you. Boy Scout," he replied. "I can also make a church out of Popsicle sticks, but that's not as useful so I don't show it off. You get the potatoes peeled?''

''They're peeled and mashed and in the oven on top of scrambled hamburger and fresh green beans. In another forty minutes it'll be shepherd's pie.''

''Sounds wonderful.'' He took a sip of the wine, then put the glass down on the coffee table and went to pick up the baby, but Shelly waved him away and took Max into her arms. He stopped crying instantly.

''I'll hold him so you can drink your wine.'' She moved to the sofa and sat down in a corner, settling Max in a sitting position in her lap. He played with a gold and silver bangle bracelet on her right hand. ''It's amazing,'' she observed, ''that at just six months old a baby's figured out that if you scream loud and long enough someone will pick up.''

He sat on the other end of the sofa. ''Babies are just like adults. Everyone wants to be held by someone who cares about them.''

No one knew that better than Shelly. She focused her attention on the baby so Connor wouldn't see that in her eyes.

''Do you think you're going to like Jester?'' she asked to divert the conversation. ''It can be pretty quiet here in the winter.''

''That's okay with me. Medicine gives me all the excitement I need.''

''What do you do with your spare time? There's good skiing not too far from here.''

He grinned. ''In L.A. I often saw the results of skiing accidents sent to us for sophisticated surgery and decided that unless I could ski in a tank, it isn't for me. I'm more of a putterer.''

"You mean…gardens and home repairs?''

He nodded. "I'm looking for a house with a shed or a garage big enough to hold a workshop.'' He sipped at his wine and looked around her living room as though checking for what should be repaired. "It's embarrassing, but at heart I'm the typical suburban guy who's happy with a house to work on, a yard to mow and bicycles to fix.''

Shelly was charmed by that revelation. He should fit well into life in Jester, where the biggest dream was to see the community thrive.

"What do you do when it's time to play?'' he asked.

"I have evenings and Sundays off, and I usually spend that time trying to catch up on the personal stuff there isn't much time for during the week.''

He frowned. "That doesn't sound restful.''

She shrugged. "I do have a cook at the restaurant who'll watch things for me if I have to leave. And during busy times, there's a high school girl I call on to help out. But mostly, I work. It's what my parents did, and it's what I've done most of my life. By the time I was six I was doing dishes and helping to clean up and prep for the next day. By the time I was ten I could replace a waitress and prepare chili or stew on my own. It was a happy life, but I worked all the time.''

He looked sympathetic. "Not precisely a child-hood."

She'd thought about that a lot and had come to what she considered a sane conclusion. "It wasn't," she agreed. "And sometimes when I was an adolescent or a teen I was resentful that other kids could play base-ball in the park or go to the movies while I was chop-ping vegetables and waiting on tables. But I realized early in high school that one of my friends was always free to do what she wanted because her mother didn't really care where she was, and another one got to do all kinds of things I couldn't because she had a little brother who had leukemia and her parents were so busy with him, they didn't worry much about her. So I got over my resentment."

"Nobody's life is perfect," he agreed. "My father was a brilliant researcher in oncology, and my mother a pediatrician. They were warm and loving, but I sel-dom saw them. I had my own resentments, then I felt guilty because I knew they were out saving the world and finally decided to just appreciate what I had. But I think it's okay to admit that you wish things had been a little different. It isn't disloyal, it's just healthy."

"I know," she agreed with a self-deprecating smile. "I just value their memory so much, I don't want them to guess even now that the life they worked so hard at deprived me of a few things. Are your parents gone?"

"My father is," he said. "My mom just retired and is living in Arizona with her sister."

"Have you been to visit?"

"Haven't had time so far."

She nodded. "Makes you almost understand how they got so busy, doesn't it?"

Curiously, he hadn't made that connection. Did that suggest he was unconsciously engaging in payback? He didn't think so. He had really been busy with his work, with two nights of call a week and every other weekend, then with the divorce and relocating. Of course, he'd had time to visit Nathan here in Jester over the summer. He would have been able to make it home.

Dinner was the best meal he'd had since he'd started driving west a week ago. He entertained the baby while Shelly cleaned up, then helped her bathe him, give him a bottle and put him to sleep.

She gave Connor the bedroom off the kitchen and put the baby down in a large quilt-lined basket in her room upstairs.

"Now, don't second-guess my question," he said, seeing three other empty rooms upstairs, "but shouldn't I be up here, too, if my purpose is to help you with him tonight?"

She laughed lightly. "I wouldn't second-guess that question. I know we're not each other's type. If he's just fussy, I think I can handle that, and if you were on call last night, you probably could use some sleep tonight. I agreed to this mostly to placate Luke, who was so determined to make peace between us.''

He didn't know whether to be annoyed or amused. On one hand, while she was probably right about their having little in common, it offended his male pride to be dismissed so easily, and on the other, if this was the first night she'd ever spent with a young baby, she was in for a few surprises about how easily it could be handled.

He knew what he'd *like* to do about the first issue, but that would be counterproductive because she was right. They weren't each other's type—though his body didn't seem to understand that. The second issue, he'd just have to let her see for herself.

"Okay, then," he said. "I'll just see that the fire's out and go to bed. And I'll lock the front door."

She nodded and offered her hand, Max asleep on her shoulder in the other arm. "Thanks for picking up those things on the way home."

"Sure."

"I'm usually out of here by five-thirty because I open at six, so come down to the restaurant when you're up and I'll give you breakfast. Okay?"

"Okay. Thank you. And thanks for dinner."

She nodded and headed upstairs while he went to the living room to kill the fire.

IT WASN'T EVEN MIDNIGHT when Shelly woke Connor the first time. "I think he's choking!" she said urgently, shaking him awake.

He was out of bed in a flash and chasing her up the stairs, expecting to find a blue-lipped baby gasping for air.

She'd moved Max from the basket to her bed where he lay on his back. His little arms were spread out and he was breathing rhythmically. Connor sat beside him and put a hand to his chest.

"He's snoring, Shelly," he said, all his adrenaline coming to a stop and puddling in the middle of his stomach. He noticed that the side of the bed on which he sat was still warm from her body.

"Babies don't snore," she said, then winced. "Do they?"

"They do. Particularly if they've had a cold."

"You mean he's fine?"

"Yes."

She sighed. "I'm sorry. I thought something was terribly wrong."

He smiled. "It's okay. That's why I'm here. Good night."

"Good night."

It was almost two when she woke him the second time. She had Max in her arms and he was screaming bloody murder.

"He's been crying for almost an hour," she said desperately. Her hair was tumbled, her eyes red, the shoulders of her robe hanging down to her elbows. "I don't know what to do! I've changed his diaper, I've tried to give him a bottle, I've rocked him until I'm dizzy. You're *sure* he's just teething?"

Connor blessed the days of residency and the nights on call that allowed him to wake out of a deep sleep relatively sharp.

He swung his legs out of bed and stood, then took Max from her. He leaned him backward in his arms, supporting his head, and thought that he looked fine, if a little pink-cheeked. He was slightly warm, but teething could make babies feverish. The textbooks denied it, but mothers swore to it. He touched his index finger to the tiny bottom lip and rubbed the little buds of teeth pushing through red and angry gums.

"Yes," he said, walking toward the kitchen. "If you'll put on some coffee, I'll see if I can get him to sleep."

"He won't sleep," she said. "I've tried everything."

"Yeah, but you're not another guy. He may just have issues only another man would understand. You know. Women, the state of the NFL, clicker control."

She looked puzzled for an instant, then asked in surprise, "You're joking? How can you be joking? I just woke you out of a deep sleep for the second time tonight, and he's screaming in your ear!"

"I'm a pediatrician," he reminded her. "Some little critter is always screaming in my ear." She stood in front of the refrigerator and he pushed her gently aside to reach into the freezer for the teething ring he'd bought along with the diapers and other things. He'd put it in the freezer after dinner. "This might help."

He put the ring in the baby's mouth. Max shook his head, trying to avoid the cold stick pacifier.

"I told you," Shelly said, filling the coffee carafe with water.

"Have faith. It'll take him a minute to realize it makes his gums feel better. Come on, sport. You're going to like this." He paced the kitchen, patting Max's back, waiting for a widemouthed scream that would allow him to insert the teething stick again.

Max rejected it again, and Connor paced and patted and just kept trying. The baby finally took it into his mouth and bit down, holding the cold plastic there. By the time the coffee was ready, Max was quiet, though wide-awake.

"I should have bet money on it," Connor said with a grin as Shelly put a steaming mug in front of him but out of the baby's reach. "You'd owe me big."

"I'll pay you anyway," she said, falling into the chair opposite him with her own cup. "Bet or no bet. I'm a complete failure with him. It's a good thing it's only for one night."

"You're just inexperienced," he corrected.

"But isn't there maternal instinct? I don't seem to have it. I mean, I feel I have it because I hurt for him and I *want* to make him feel better, but instinct doesn't tell me what to do."

"It would if you had time with him. It's like all relationships. You have to get to know each other to know how to help."

She took a sip of coffee, her expression dispirited.

She leaned her chin in her hand and looked at him as though he were an interesting specimen. "Is that what made you become a pediatrician? Wanting to get to know children?"

"It was an accidental thing," he said, sitting Max on his knee and rubbing his back as the baby played with his watch. "I went to school, intending to be a neurosurgeon, make a fortune and retire early. But in my pediatrics rotation, I fell in love with children. They're courageous, resilient, ever hopeful and fun to watch. Unless things go bad, and then it's the worst kind of hell for all involved."

She could see that he meant that in all sincerity. Unable to think about dying children, she diverted the conversation.

"I suppose neurosurgery requires that you live in a big city near a major medical center. I mean, it isn't something you could do from Jester."

He nodded. "That's about right."

"And you probably won't get to retire early here."

"I know. But that's all right. Lisa wanted that more than I did."

"Lisa?"

"My ex-wife. She left when I made the switch to pediatrics."

Max began to fuss and whine. Connor stood him up on his knees so that he could look around. The baby stopped crying and studied Shelly with interest. She made faces and the baby laughed. Connor laughed, too.

Shelly sobered and shook her head at Connor. "I'm sorry. It must be hard to lose someone because of the change in a dream you once had in common."

"Oh," he said with a sigh, "by the time all was said and done, it was pretty clear that her interest in me was more dependent upon what I could give her than what we could do together. She wanted to be a clothing designer and she told me, in a fit of anger as she was packing, that my income was supposed to support that." Max began to fuss again and Connor put him to his shoulder and grinned. "That diminished my grief considerably."

"How awful."

"It wasn't so bad. I was probably as much to blame. I thought having a beautiful woman on my arm was a measure of success. And in trying to fill that spot, I mistook sexual attraction for love. Hard to blame someone else for that. But I'm doing fine on my own for now."

"But you want children," she reminded him.

"Maybe I'll just adopt a few."

That was possible, of course, but sounded as though it could fall short of the goal of family. "I know that's the perfect solution in some situations, and if you have no choice but to be a one-parent family, then you deal with that. But family should be about two people loving and nurturing the children they either made together, or invited into their lives together."

He focused on her in mild surprise. "I thought you didn't want children?"

"I don't." She thought about that a minute, as though she'd surprised herself. "But you do. I just think if you're intending to make that kind of move in your life, you should do it in the right way." Then she sighed and stood. "Why am I telling *you* what to do? I must be tired."

He stood, too, Max now sound asleep on his shoulder. "Want me to keep him with me for the rest of the night?" he asked. "You haven't gotten much sleep."

"No." She replied firmly and took the baby carefully from him. "People's lives are in your hands. If I mess up a burger, nobody dies." She added with a grin, "Well, hopefully. Good night."

Max was awake and screaming before she was halfway up the stairs, but she kept going, determined to get him back to sleep on her own.

He finally drifted off twenty minutes later out of sheer exhaustion. She tried to do the same but seemed to have reached a point where sleep was no longer even possible.

A few hours later, with Max's carrier in a shadowy corner of the kitchen, Shelly made him a bottle, packed the diaper-bag-briefcase and the sack of things Connor had brought into the car, then, with a hand on the carrier in the passenger seat, drove the one block to the coffee shop and unloaded everything.

Dan was already there, warming the grill, slicing fruit, putting away last night's final load of clean crockery. He came to help her with the baby.

"About that check, Shelly," he began, apparently prepared to argue. "That was very generous of you, but I think you should make sure you'll have enough to—"

"I'm sure." She pulled off her coat. "Dan, you've done so much for me over the years, personally and professionally, that I couldn't begin to show my appreciation in ways that really count. So…the check."

"But, you…"

"I don't want to hear any more about it, okay? Just do something fun with it."

"Shelly…"

She put a finger to her lips. "Don't wake the baby or I'll take the check back."

He finally smiled and gave her an awkward hug. "Thank you. How come you've still got him anyway?" Dan asked, putting the carrier on a corner of the counter.

She explained about Luke being unable to reach Pine Run, and the new pediatrician spending the night at her place.

He raised an eyebrow. "I'm surprised you didn't self-destruct with a man that close."

She made a face at him. "I have a lot of male friends, and you know it."

"Friends, yes. Men who sleep over, no."

"He stayed because I have no experience with babies and he hasn't found a place to live yet. It was Luke's idea."

"Yeah, but I've met the doc. Nice guy. Isn't it time

you got serious about what women are really meant for?''

She froze to stare at him with a horrified expression, pulling off her scarf. ''Daniel Bertram. I can't believe what I'm hearing! I thought you were more enlightened than that. Your daughter wants to be an aeronautical engineer, for heaven's sake. And you're going to stand there and tell me a woman's destiny is to satisfy a man?''

''No,'' he replied, rocking the carrier as the baby shifted fitfully. ''I'm telling you, her destiny is to love a man, so he can love her in return. Each achieves the most, personally and professionally, while in a devoted relationship. And if there's great lovemaking involved, that's all to the good.''

She carried her coat to the small office in the back, then returned, tying on a blue cobbler apron patterned in snowflakes.

''I'm committed to this place, just like my parents were,'' she said. ''It doesn't leave much time for anything else.''

''There's always time for something else,'' he insisted, straightening carefully away when the baby quieted. He lowered his voice. ''Work is stimulating and fulfilling, but love is the reason we endure.'' He smiled wistfully. ''And sometimes it's just the memory of love. But if it was good, it's enough.'' He patted her on the shoulder as he walked back to the grill. ''Get yourself some before it's too late.''

Chapter Four

Shelly glanced at the clock above the counter. Almost six o'clock. She was on time for the regulars who would be arriving any moment, but she was too late for love. She'd built a life around The Brimming Cup and the people of Jester. This was her world. There wasn't room for anything else. Except for the occasional trip, now that she had the means.

Dean Kenning arrived just after six, newspaper under his arm, and greeted her with a cheerful "Good morning!" as she poured him a cup of coffee. His habit was to take his cup to the booth on the window side at the farthest end of the restaurant where his cronies would soon be joining him. They would discuss world events, the sad state of baseball today, and the oppressive presence of the press in Jester. They'd been meeting here every morning since Shelly was a child, and discussing the same issues, though the presence of the press was something new.

But this morning, he was waylaid by the sight of the baby carrier.

"What's this?" he asked Shelly. Then he shouted toward Dan, "You get some girl pregnant, Dan, and she left you the baby?"

"Ha! Ha!" Dan replied. "Thanks for your faith in me. Over or scrambled?"

"Over. And bacon. I've got a big day ahead of me." He refocused his attention on Shelly, who came to touch the sleeping baby and tell Dean his story.

He nodded. "So that's why the doc spent the night at your place." He waggled his eyebrows. "I was hoping it was passion and lewd behavior."

She gave him a punitive glance. "Nothing of the sort. It was mixing formula and walking the floors. And how did you know Dr. O'Rourke stayed with me?"

"Saw his car in front of your place when I left the Heartbreaker at one o'clock this morning. All the lights were out."

"Well, that must have been one of the rare moments when we were sleeping—separately," she added with emphasis, "because the baby kept us up most of the night."

He nodded philosophically. "I guess they do that. Cute little guy." He gave the sleeping baby a smile, then went to the back booth.

It was impossible to tell by looking at Dean that he was now a millionaire. Of course, she was, too, and she looked the same as she had yesterday. Excitement rippled inside her at the thought. The baby had so consumed her attention yesterday and this morning that she'd almost forgotten her good fortune. She was a millionaire!

She was enjoying the thought when Luke walked in, his shoulders and his hat frosted with snow. He went straight to the carrier as Shelly poured his coffee and placed it on the counter where he always sat, second stool from the end.

"How'd he do last night?" he asked softly. Then he caught Shelly's eye and winced. "You don't look as though you did very well."

Her eyes burned and she felt hungover, though the strongest thing she'd had to drink was diet cola.

She placed a little bowl of creamers near his coffee cup and smiled flatly into his face as he swept off his hat and straddled the stool. "Someone thought it would be a good idea if I kept Max overnight. So I didn't get much sleep."

"Wasn't the doc any help?"

"He was the only reason I got the hour or two I did get."

"I'm sorry." Luke sipped his coffee and made a sound of approval. "I promise I'll get through to Pine Run today if I have to ride the snowplow over."

"That would be good, Luke. You having a waffle this morning?"

"Yeah. One egg and a side of sausage."

She called the order back to Dan and hung the ticket on the wheel.

Several reporters came in along with Henry Faulkner, who'd once owned the hardware store but was now retired, and Sylvia Rutledge, who owned the hair salon. Both were now Main Street Millionaires also. Henry went to the back booth to sit with Dean.

The morning rush was on. It was half an hour later before there was enough of a lull that she could stop and look around to assess the situation. She took the coffeepot in one hand and the water pitcher in the other and started her rounds.

She noticed odd behavior in the back booth. And several odd glances at the counter. Sylvia had passed Luke the front page of the *Plain Talker* in a curiously surreptitious way. Shelly ignored it, thinking they were probably just discussing another front-page article about the Main Street Millionaires.

Then she saw Dean and his cronies muttering and grinning as they watched her approach, table by table, then a mad scrambling to hide the newspaper as she reached them.

"What's going on?" she asked, ignoring the cups held out toward her.

"Nothing," Henry replied innocently. "Why would something be going on?"

"You've all been watching me."

"Well, you're gorgeous, Shell, you know that," Finn Hollis replied. He was a retired librarian and the third member of the back-booth triumvirate. "We're all a little bit in love with you."

"Yeah, yeah." She rolled her eyes, still withholding coffee. "Why did you hide the newspaper?"

"Oh…" Dean stammered, "We…ah…we know

you're just tired of articles about the lottery and we…''

Dean was turning red. He always turned red when he lied about the fish he'd caught, the woman he visited regularly in Pine Run, the money he won in Tahoe. And he was lying again.

"Let me see it," she insisted.

Dean held his cup right up to the spout of the coffeepot she held away. "Please, Shelly. We're just a bunch of hardworking guys and we can't start the day without…"

She held firm. "I want to see the paper."

Dean put his cup on the table and held a hand up to Finn, who had scrambled to conceal it. Finn handed it to Dean, who held it up so that Shelly could read the headline.

Jackpot Baby Finds Millionaire Momma, it said in bold block print. Then underneath in slightly smaller print, the subhead read, Handsome Houseguest Makes It Three.

Shelly gasped and fell into a chair just opposite the booth to read the article. It had been written by Harvey Brinkman. She put aside thoughts of murder to concentrate on his copy.

Shelly Dupree, owner of Jester's The Brimming Cup and one of its Main Street Millionaires, returned to the coffee shop Wednesday afternoon after depositing her lottery winnings to find an abandoned baby on the counter. The baby is a six-month-old named Max who appears to be in perfect health, except for a slight fever Dr. Connor O'Rourke suspects is related to teething.

O'Rourke joined the Jester Medical Center staff on Saturday. He graduated cum laude from the UCLA School of Medicine in Westwood, California, where he met Nathan Perkins, director of the center. He is a family practitioner with a specialty in pediatrics.

Ms. Dupree, known around the county for her Dutch apple pie and her sunny disposition, was asked by Sheriff Luke McNeil to take the baby home when he was unable to contact Child and Family Services in Pine Run. Telephone service was down again due to the storm. Ray Livingstone, director of Canyon Telephone, promises that service will be back on line by the end of the week. Efforts are also being made to import cellular telephone towers so that this service may be enjoyed with some dependability by the consumers of northeastern Montana.

The good doctor volunteered to spend the night with Ms. Dupree to help care for the foundling. It's a comfort to know that the good doctor comes to Fallon County not only with impressive credentials but with a generous nature, as well.

So far there is no information on the identity of the baby's natural mother.

Shelly folded the paper carefully, then smacked Dean on the arm with it before handing it back. She heard herself emit a high-pitched shriek of complete exasperation. "Of all the tabloid-reeking, sensation-seeking, inaccurate, completely unnewsworthy…!"

The bell over the front door rang as Connor walked into the coffee shop. She could see from across the room that his eyes were as bleary as hers, though they lent him a sort of smoldering sexuality that stopped the words in her throat. She saw that her morning paper was rolled up in his fist like a telescope.

So, he'd read it, too. He must be furious, she thought. He must want to kill her, and then the reporter, and then whoever had given him that information. Her money was on the pretty little receptionist at the medical center.

Everyone who'd been staring at Shelly while she had her tirade had now shifted their attention to him. He tossed the paper on the counter, scanned the room and spotted her standing with the coffeepot near the back booth.

She hurried toward him, babbling. "I'm so sorry! I've called the paper on the reporter so many times, and he's been censured over and over, but he's got this tattletale-news mentality and he's just impossible to stop!" She lowered her voice as she drew closer and saw the intensity of emotion banked in his eyes. "I'll take care of everything. I know this isn't the kind of impression you wanted to make your first week here. God knows I've worked hard to preserve my…"

CONNOR WAS SURE she was about to tell him that she'd worked hard to preserve her reputation, and for reasons he couldn't quite define, that sent him over the edge.

He'd had a long, sleepless night, and it hadn't been entirely the baby's fault. The first time Shelly had awakened him last night, she'd donned a robe and their conversation had been relatively brief.

The second time, however, she'd been upset and forgotten the robe. She'd awakened him wearing a thigh-length flannel shirt, and though it had been too voluminous to show him any detail of her breasts and hips, the fabric had clung occasionally, suggesting curves and hollows and making him desperate for a glimpse.

He'd looked into her sleepy hazel eyes and talked about babies and families while feeling lonesome for familiar things. Then she'd taken the baby from him and walked away on bare, slender legs—an image that had haunted him until he heard her get up again and prepare to leave.

He'd wanted to get up, too, but he didn't want to do anything to draw her attention. At least until he'd had a cold shower.

Then he'd read the news story and laughed.

He'd come into the restaurant to ask her if she wanted him to take the baby to the center, where he'd be certain to sleep more comfortably, and he heard her hotly denying the veracity of the story, desperate to make her customers believe that their night together had been innocent.

It had, but it annoyed him to see the desperation in her eyes as she tried to explain. Irritated him that she was certain he'd be angry about the news story and was trying to placate him with promises of vindication.

And it really ticked him off that she could walk up to him this morning, look into his eyes and reveal nothing of the sexual frustration he felt after spending the night in the same house with her.

Something inside him demanded that he change that.

He wrapped an arm around her waist, pulled her to him with one deft yank and, as her eyes widened in astonishment and her lips parted in a little cry of surprise, he kissed her with all the emotion roiling up in him. He felt her resist for an instant, then soften, and every instinct he had for persuasion went into his efforts.

He heard gasps from the women and shouts of encouragement from the men. When he eventually freed her mouth and took a step back, Shelly was limp in his arms. The place was silent.

She finally seemed to come to and opened her eyes with an angry snap. He kissed her once again quickly, briefly.

"I'll take Max to the center with me," he said, catching the handle of the carrier. "See you at home tonight."

He took great pleasure in walking away with the

baby as she stared at him with her mouth agape, all her customers whistling and applauding.

He was not at all surprised when she burst in on him on his coffee break. It was late morning and he'd already treated a broad variety of ailments in the older population, stitched a big toe and a left forearm, and sent a compound fracture to the hospital in Pine Run.

Max was awake and they sat together on a blanket on the floor in the upstairs storage room while Connor ate the peanut butter sandwich he'd made at Shelly's and Max played with a little rubber duck that squeaked.

She barged in without knocking, her coat hanging open over the cobbler apron that covered her jeans and a white sweater. She'd put on lipstick, he noted. It was a raspberry color that seemed to brighten her cheeks, as well.

"What were you *doing?*" she demanded as she strode into the room and stood in front of him. The baby shook the duck madly in one hand and raised the other one to her.

Her expression changed from fury to delight in an instant, and she was completely distracted by the reaching baby. She bent down and lifted him into her arms.

"How are you, sweetheart?" she asked in a crooning voice. "Did you finally get some sleep? I'm sorry you have to spend the day with this horrible man."

She said that last in the same sweet voice she'd used to greet the baby.

Max hit her on the chin with the duck and laughed.

She took the duck from him and tapped him on the nose with it. He laughed again.

She wasn't a woman who didn't want children, Connor saw in a sudden glimpse of insight. She simply thought her life wouldn't allow it.

The baby took the duck from her and tossed it onto the blanket Connor had spread. She put him down to play with it. He knelt on all fours, apparently contemplating the secret to crawling.

"Why did you *do* that?" she demanded of Connor in a sharp whisper. "I was trying to avert gossip after that ridiculous bit of yellow journalism, and you come in and act like…like…"

"A man who's interested in you?" he suggested helpfully.

She angled her chin stiffly. "That was pretty emphatic for simple interest."

He smiled. "I'm glad you noticed."

She frowned at him. "What are you saying?"

He spread both arms. "I thought that was clear. I'm interested in you. More than a little."

She stammered. "I…it…what do you *mean?*" she finished in a very satisfying state of confusion.

He shrugged as though it should be clear. "I have a crush on you."

She made an impatient sound. "A crush? What do you mean, a crush? No one has crushes anymore! This is the age of one-night stands, or, if you're very discerning, sex on the third date!''

She was upset.

"Well, I moved too fast the first time I thought I was in love,'' he said honestly, "and I'm determined to do it right now that I have a second chance.''

"No,'' she said firmly. "I'm not a second chance. You do *not* have a second chance. At least not with me.''

"Come on,'' he chided. "You know that isn't true.''

"It's true! I'm telling you, it's true! I am not available! I have a business to maintain. I don't want to settle down with the children you want to have! And for the first time in my life, I have a chance to travel and do things and I'm going to take advantage of it!''

He nodded. "And you should. But why does that preclude romance?''

"Because romance is intended for the purpose of finding a permanent relationship! I am not going there.''

"I hate to be the bearer of bad news,'' he said gently, "but you *are* there. I felt the tip of your tongue when I kissed you. You put your hands to my waist and they wanted to explore. I could feel it.''

She was speechless for a moment, then she swept her hand in an arc in front of her as though trying to erase what he'd said.

"Well, it doesn't matter,'' she said finally. "This

is over today. Luke will get CFS to take the baby and I won't need your help anymore.''

"Our attraction will remain," he said, "whether or not there's a baby drawing us together. And this is a small town. We're bound to keep bumping into each other. Sooner or later you'll need a flu shot or an antibiotic or…''

Shelly was determined to nip this in the bud. She put on her most superior expression—one she'd cultivated for using on truckers or salesmen passing through who thought a small-town waitress would be eager for their attentions.

"If I need medical help," she said coolly, "I'll go to Pine Run. And I'm sure the fact that I've just banked over a million dollars has contributed substantially to my attraction for you. I'm not an idiot, Connor.''

She'd expected that accusation to either anger him or offend him. She was surprised when he appeared to be amused instead.

"While it's true that I'm not a millionaire," he said, "my father left me a substantial inheritance, which I've invested wisely, and though pediatrics doesn't pay as well as neurosurgery, Nathan made me an attractive offer to relocate to Jester. I made a lump-sum settlement with Lisa when we sold the house we shared, so I'm not paying alimony and I have no children to support. And no restaurant. I probably have more disposable income than you do.''

Annoyed that she'd not only *not* upset him, but

given him ammunition to turn on her, she angled her chin and, after a gentle pat on Max's head, turned for the door. Connor caught her arm and stopped her.

"And another thing."

She rolled her eyes. "What?"

"You *are* an idiot," he said, looking into her eyes, "if you think that money is the most appealing thing about you." He freed her and walked around her to open the door.

She sailed though it without another word.

She didn't like him, she thought, storming back toward the coffee shop. She should have trusted her original impression of him. And he was entirely too smooth when it suited his purposes, and determined to have things his way.

She held her coat closed against the snow and almost collided with Luke at the door to the coffee shop.

"Did you get in touch with CFS?" she demanded.

He blinked at her tone of voice, than replied regretfully, "Yes, I did. Their office is short staffed because of colds and flu, and the two caseworkers remaining are swamped. I assured her the baby was in good hands until tomorrow. I checked with the doc, and he can give you another night."

"*Give* me another night?" she asked hotly.

Luke grinned. "Yeah. And I'm not surprised. I heard that kiss in the restaurant after I left was pretty hot."

After an initial impulse to punch him, she asked

instead, "And how are you doing on the search for Max's mother?"

"Nothing yet, but I'm working on it."

She marched past him into the shop, determined he would be getting his daily bowl of stew in his lap today. Then she was going to track down and do bodily harm to everyone who'd been in the coffee shop this morning and passed on the story.

She'd call Connor and tell him he could stay home tonight, that she and Max would manage just fine, but she was sure she'd regret it. He knew what he was doing with babies and she didn't. What a sorry state of affairs when a grown woman had to depend on a man to care for a little baby. Even if the man was a doctor.

Amanda Bradley was sitting at the far end of the counter when Shelly went back to work. They'd been friends since Amanda moved to Jester when she was eight, just a year older than Shelly. She'd been pretty even then, when Shelly had been all scraped knees and torn clothing. She'd since grown into a classically beautiful young woman with long, light brown hair and lively brown eyes. Today she wore a simple white silk shirt under a gray-blue vee-neck sweater and blue wool slacks. She looked like an ad for the elegant career woman as she closed her menu and tucked it behind the napkin holder.

Unlike Shelly who felt like the "before" picture in a makeover ad.

"Well, you're certainly efficient," Amanda teased

as Shelly approached her. "A million dollars, a baby, and a man who isn't embarrassed to kiss you in front of a crowd—and all in just a few days!"

Shelly pointed her pen at her. "You're on thin ice, lady. The million was a fluke, the baby was abandoned and I'm just doing my Christian duty, and the man…well, I don't know what to say about him. He's picked on me from the moment I met him, yet he kissed me in front of everyone just because he knew I'd hate it."

Amanda looked her over and smiled in question. "Did you?"

Shelly and Amanda had shared confidences since girlhood. "Not entirely," she admitted quietly. "But he's not serious and I'm not getting involved with anyone."

"Why not?" Amanda leaned over the counter toward her. "I noticed him the day he arrived in town. He came in to buy Lavinia Hollis's *History of Jester, Montana* and we talked a little bit. He seemed very sweet. And it was nice of him to stay the night so he could help you with the baby."

Shelly thought she detected a subtle teasing note in Amanda's voice but could find no evidence of it in her wide, ingenuous eyes. Lavinia Hollis had been Finn's mother, whose love of books and Jester had been her legacy to her son.

"What are you doing here—taco salad, no olives?"

"Please."

Shelly called the order back to Dan and hung the

ticket. "Someone covering for you this afternoon so I don't have to deliver your lunch?"

"Yeah. Irene's here. I just needed to get away for an hour."

Irene Caldwell was an older woman, a widow who lived at the boardinghouse and helped Amanda part-time.

"Dev's got some construction people at the Heart-breaker," Amanda went on, "and I don't know what's going on but I can't hear myself think, much less catch up on bookkeeping. Someday I'm going to take out a contract on that man."

"Can't you just stick your head in the door and ask him to keep it down?"

Amanda made a face. "I get my head anywhere near him and he bites it off. Besides, my rabies shot isn't current."

Shelly shook her head sympathetically. "A book-store and a saloon just shouldn't share the same building. But since you have to, it seems as though the two of you could find some way to coexist instead of arguing all the time."

"He doesn't want to get along. He just wants to get rid of me by buying my half of the building. And I won't do it!"

"Because *you* don't want to, or because it would make him happy?"

"I inherited it!" Amanda said hotly. "I shouldn't have to leave!"

"Okay, okay," Shelly placated. "I just hate to see

you so upset all the time. I don't know what to do for you.''

Amanda sighed and gave her a wistful smile. ''You've done something without knowing it. I love the thought of a strange man giving me a passionate kiss in front of everyone. If it happened to you, maybe it can happen to me.'' Then she seemed to call herself back to reality. ''In the meantime, get me my taco salad and a large double mocha and I'll be happy.''

''Coming right up.''

Shelly was cleaning up after closing and Dan had already left when she noticed through the window what looked like a wolf or a coyote approaching the Dumpster at the back of the coffee shop. She'd been hearing about him for a week, and saw him for the first time a few days ago when she carried out the garbage. He'd run for cover the minute she opened the door. He was acquiring a reputation around town as a menace rooting through garbage cans. The rumor was that Jester was being stalked by a wolf.

He was gray-brown in color with the lean, hungry look of a wolf. But there was something ''unprofessional'' looking about his sniff and perusal of the Dumpster that suggested he wasn't a wolf at all, but a dog. He found a crust of bread that had fallen to the snow and ate it hungrily, but started to run when a piece of paper fluttered past. If he had to get by on his heroism, he'd never make it. She guessed, watching him skulk back to where he'd found the bread,

that he was a dog and not a wolf, and that he'd probably once been someone's pet.

She went to the refrigerator for scraps of trimmed
fat and beef bones that she saved for various customers' dogs, and put half of them in a bowl. Then she
went out the back door and watched the dog run off
into the trees. She put the bowl down near the Dumpster and tried to call him back, but he was out of sight
and was apparently unwilling to show his face.

She hurried back inside and waited at the window
for him to reappear. He waited a long moment, then
came slowly, stealthily, into the floodlit back of the
restaurant, picking up his pace as he caught a whiff
of the meat scraps. He scarfed them quickly, raising
his head occasionally to check for intruders.

He licked the bowl clean, looked around, probably
longing for more, grabbed the bone, then ran off.

Shelly's heart went out to him. The lost look in his
eyes reminded her of how she sometimes felt—alone
and adrift. Her friends were wonderful, but there had
to be something more to the future than work and
civic responsibilities.

But if there were, that would be change, wouldn't
it? And she didn't think she wanted that.

God, she thought, making sure all the appliances
were off, then turning out the kitchen light, life was
getting complicated and she hadn't even yet given serious thought to what to do with her money.

Maybe she should get input from her customers.
The thought struck her like a lightbulb going on, even

as she physically turned off lights. She'd take a poll, collect suggestions, make it a community affair!

As she came around the counter, she saw Connor standing with Max in his arms just outside the door. She unlocked it and let him in. He smelled deliciously of the cold outdoors.

"Hi," he said. "Ready to go home?"

Just the sight of his handsome face and the memory of this morning's kiss made her feel irascible. "It's my home," she said, flipping off the lights behind the counter. "Not yours."

"I know. It's just the kind of place a lonely bachelor dreams about."

Now she felt guilty for her mean response.

"You don't really have to stay with us," she said, taking Max from him. "I'll be all right and I'm sure you have better things to do."

"No, I don't," he corrected. "I'd be happy to help you with Max again. He caught up on his sleep today while we were busy, so he'll probably be awake for hours."

"You're asking for another sleepless night. I tried hard, but I don't seem to have the knack for getting him back to sleep when he wakes up."

He shrugged. "Maybe we'll get lucky. Come on. Nathan lent us a car seat. I'll drive us home."

She caught his arm as he turned toward the door. "You don't think *you're* going to get lucky tonight because I let you kiss me today?"

He raised an eyebrow, a small smile forming on his

lips. "I don't 'get lucky' in that way. When it happens, it's romantic energy and skill. It has nothing to do with luck."

Her lips parted in a soundless gasp.

"And you didn't let me kiss you, I just did it. And with just the smallest—though very promising—cooperation on your part. The next move is yours."

"I'm not going to make it," she said, both amazed at and admiring of his arrogance. "So don't come home with me thinking I will."

"I'm a patient man."

"You'll have to be eternally patient."

"You underestimate my charms."

She didn't want to smile, but she couldn't help herself. So to try to convince him that her amusement had nothing to do with him, she smiled at the briefcase hanging from his shoulder. "It's a shame Nathan couldn't also lend us a diaper bag."

Connor laughed lightly. "It's all right. I don't have anything to take back and forth to work with me here. No complicated case files to study. I had packed some favorite books in it when I moved, so it was handy when we needed something. And when I'm carrying it, I feel less ridiculous than I would in a light blue diaper bag covered with baby ducks or something."

She had to giggle at that image. But nothing, she thought, stepping past him onto the sidewalk and noticing how angular he was—chin, shoulders, big square hands—could diminish the impression he made of serious masculinity.

"Actually, I drove this morning," she said, very much aware of him and happy she had an alternative to being confined with him in his car. "I had a lot to carry. I'll meet you at home."

His eyes held hers, filled with amusement. She suspected he knew how she was feeling. "You said it *wasn't* my home."

"Oh, shut up." She turned away from him and headed for her car, parked at the end of the block.

Chapter Five

As Connor built a fire in the fireplace, he noted that the aroma of dinner underway, whatever it was, smelled wonderful. They followed the same procedure that had worked the night before—he kept Max entertained while Shelly prepared dinner.

He'd tried to argue with her about that, certain that after an entire day spent cooking and waiting tables, fixing dinner was the last thing she'd want to do. But she insisted she was preparing something special, and that she found it relaxing to cook things she never made for the restaurant.

He couldn't imagine that, but spent the hour she worked in the kitchen trying to exhaust the baby so that he'd let them sleep tonight. He bounced Max on his knee, held him up above his head while he giggled loudly, played with his toys, rolled a ball, then finally lay in front of the fire with a yawning Max on his chest.

"I hate to disturb you," Shelly said quietly, "but dinner's served."

"That's okay," he replied in the same tone. "I think he's down for the count—for a while, anyway."

He put Max in the carrier and brought it with him into the kitchen and placed it on the counter.

He looked in pleased surprise at the colorful and aromatic chicken dish with wild rice and baby carrots in the middle of the table. The table had been set with candles and the napkins folded like fountains in the wineglasses.

"Chicken Provençale," she announced.

"Wow," he said appreciatively. "Are we celebrating something?"

She began to shake her head, then seemed to change her mind. "Actually, I think we are." She sat, so he did, too. "I've been wondering what to do with the portion of my money I want to use to help Jester. And it just occurred to me as I was closing up tonight that I should take a poll at the restaurant. Have everybody write down their suggestions. What do you think?" She passed him a basket of butter-flake rolls.

He took one, then accepted the butter dish from her. "It's hard to find fault with that. And it's generous of you to want to share your winnings. But I thought you said you wanted to take advantage of the opportunity to travel."

"I do. It's just that Jester needs help. We haven't been prosperous in so long that I don't know where to start. Whatever I do, I want to make it count."

"Maybe you should just take a walk around town and give it some thought. See what you think needs help, then have your customers vote for which seems most worthy. With the people's input, it'll certainly count.''

"I was thinking about something like that.''

"I'll come with you,'' he volunteered. "Take notes. It'll be good for me to learn what's valuable to the people of Jester.''

She was less enthused about that idea. So he withheld mention of the notion he had of renting a room from her on a more permanent basis.

She served cheesecake with blueberry sauce for dessert. "I love this stuff,'' she said. "I always buy two for the restaurant, and one for me.''

"You going to enlarge the restaurant?'' he asked, marveling at the gourmet meal he'd just enjoyed in a remote little town in the boondocks. "I'll bet that chicken Provençale would make you a fortune.''

She shook her head. "I tried it. It doesn't fly here. Not because my customers are unsophisticated, but because they're used to simple fare and that's what they prefer. You can't explain the benefits of eating according to the healthy food pyramid to guys like Dean or Finn. They don't want to hear it. I tried a few pasta dishes at lunch and ended up eating it myself. My introduction of chicken Provençale, cioppino and scampi was met with a resounding 'What happened to the chicken strips?'''

Despite that explanation, her cheeks were still flushed from the time she'd spent cooking, her eyes still bright with the pleasure of serving it. "Then...

what about a fine-dining restaurant someplace else? Billings? Helena?''

She shrugged. "I love it here."

He wondered about that. He leaned back in his chair, knowing he had to approach this carefully. "Maybe it's more that you're comfortable here. In order to stretch your talents, you might have to reach out of what's familiar into what seems scary."

"I have a long history here," she said reasonably. "I'm friends with the kids of the people my parents were friends with."

"And that's great. But if it stops you from doing what you really want to do, history should take a back seat to change. You're too young to base your life on the past."

She looked confused by his arguments, and surprised him by pouring each of them another glass of wine and leaning toward him conspiratorially. "Why is it," she asked, toasting him with her glass, "that you're encouraging me to leave Jester, when you just moved here and insist that you're interested in me?"

She had him there. What *was* he doing?

"I thought you'd commute," he said.

She gasped a laugh. "To Helena? That's almost four hundred miles."

"You're a millionaire," he joked. "You can buy a plane."

She teased him with a look before taking another sip of wine. "If I'm expected to commute because you're courting me, *you* can buy the plane."

"If that's the condition of a deal," he said, holding his glass toward hers, "pick one out tomorrow."

She stared at him, clearly trying to decide whether or not he was serious. "You're a complete nut," she said finally, rising to clear the table.

He thought it a pity that the deal went unsealed.

He helped her clean up, then when she headed for the back door with a bag of trash, he took it from her. She went to flip on the porch light for him, but nothing happened.

"Sorry. Bulb must have burned out." She held the door open wide so he could see the trash can by the kitchen light.

"You need a handyman," he teased. "Put him in the courtship deal, and I'll pay for him, too."

MAX SLEPT until three in the morning. Connor heard his cries and Shelly's quiet attempts to soothe him. Her footsteps padded into the kitchen, and her quiet voice spoke to the crying baby while she opened the freezer. He knew she was looking for the pacifier. It was in his jacket pocket.

He pulled on his jeans and went out into the kitchen. She'd forgotten the robe again and he was treated to the sight of her long, gorgeous legs, her feet on tiptoe as she groped around in the freezer, trying to hold the crying baby away from the blast of cold air.

He held up the pacifier to show her that he had it. "Sorry," he said. "I intended to put it in the freezer when we got home, and forgot. I noticed you had Popsicles. Let's try one of those."

She looked at him wide-eyed. "Seriously?"

"Sure. Cut it off to a stub, put a bib on him, and I'll get him back to sleep. You go back to bed."

"Do I have to remind you that lives are in your hands at the center? You have to be rested."

"Not tomorrow. I have the day off so I can sleep in. Go to bed."

She vacillated.

"Get me a Popsicle," he said firmly, "then go."

She retrieved an orange-flavored Popsicle, closed the freezer door, then faced him with her free hand on her hip. "If you intend to carry on a courtship, or indulge a crush, or whatever it is you think you're doing," she advised, "I'd lighten up the orders."

He was probably stupid to consider the remark hopeful, but he did. He had a feeling she wasn't entirely kidding.

"I appreciate that information," he said. While her eyes seemed to be ensnared by his, he took pleasure in maintaining the spell a moment longer. Then he pointed to the Popsicle she held. "We need that before it melts."

With a murderous slice of a knife, she cut the top off it, handed him the stick, and headed toward the stairs with a yawn.

He heard her tiptoe to the doorway of his room at shortly after five. She was dressed in jeans and a green sweater that did magical things to her eyes. He propped himself up on an elbow, Max asleep on the mattress beside him.

"Everything okay?" she whispered.

"Fine," he replied. "You off to work?"

"Yes. And the coffee shop's open for dinner tonight, so I'll be late. I'll call Luke and tell him Max is home with you today. If…if the caseworker from Pine Run comes for him, will you call me?"

"Of course."

"You're welcome to come to the shop for meals today."

"Thanks. Maybe I'll come for dinner."

"Okay. Have a good day." She started to leave, then turned back. "Oh. And I forgot to mention that my father had a shop in the garage. If you want to putter with the tools or anything, feel free."

That was exactly what he'd do with his day—as much as Max would allow.

He blew her a kiss.

She stared at him a moment, began to return the gesture, then stopped halfway. With one final worried look at him, she hurried through the kitchen and out the door.

JACK HARTMAN, Jester's veterinarian, walked into The Brimming Cup and quickly closed the door behind him. He was tall and broad shouldered in a brown canvas barn jacket, a handsome widower who'd lost his wife and their unborn child five years ago. Shelly had heard rumors that since he'd become one of the

Main Street Millionaires many of the local single women were determined to change his marital status.

He flattened himself against the wall, then peered through the window as though checking to see if he was being followed.

"Oh, jeez!" he exclaimed, and turned to Shelly with an urgent expression. "Can you hide me?"

She was taken aback by the question for an instant, then gestured him behind the counter. "Duck down back here. What's wrong?"

"You'll see in a minute," he whispered.

He'd just spoken the words when the door flew open and Paula Pratt stood there, her tiny beige Chihuahua clutched against her bosom. It occurred to Shelly that he could smother there if Paula wasn't careful.

"Is Jack here?" she asked, remaining in the doorway. "I thought I saw him come this way."

All the midmorning regulars—Dean and his cronies, Amanda, who'd come to pick up her mocha, Luke, and Sylvia Rutledge from the beauty shop—pretended interest in their food or the menu, though she caught them glancing up to watch the action.

Shelly tried to avoid a lie. "Something wrong with Killer?"

Paula stroked the dog's trembling head. He always looked to Shelly as though he was in the throes of a convulsion or some eye-bugging thyroid attack. Paula, she guessed, could do that to a person—or a dog.

"His eyes are cloudy and he's listless." She stated

those symptoms in a kind of whine. She seemed to Shelly to have different personalities depending on which man she was trying to impress. Bobby, who needed strength in a woman, brought out her efficient handmaiden personality. But Jack, who was all man and then some—except, of course, at the moment as he cowered behind the counter—turned her into a helpless female. "I ran home on my coffee break to bring him in to see Jack."

"Isn't Melinda there?" Shelly asked. "I know she's new to the vet clinic, but Sean Connery likes her."

Paula made a petulant face. "Robert doesn't like her. None of the guys do."

"Well, maybe they're not being fair. Why don't you go see for yourself?"

She sighed. The dog, resting on her bosom, went up and down like a surfer on a wave. "I'll try again at lunch." And she stepped back onto the sidewalk and closed the door behind her.

Jack tried to stand, but Shelly held his head down.

"Wait," she said. "She's standing out front, deciding what to do."

"Jack Hartman, you are such a coward," Amanda teased with a laugh. "Can't you just tell her you're not interested?"

"Have you ever tried to reason with Paula Pratt?" he asked from his crouched position.

Shelly, watching Paula run across the street to her

eggplant PT Cruiser, rapped lightly on his head as a signal that the coast was clear. "Okay. She's gone."

Jack got to his feet with a groan. He looked tired.

"You're not dealing with a sleepless baby, too, are you?" Shelly poured him a cup of coffee and reached into the counter-top covered plate for the apple Danish he always had midmorning.

He went around the counter to take his customary place. "No, just very determined females. Mary Kay Thompson was there to meet me this morning when I opened the clinic. She has this giant marmalade tabby she keeps trying to tell me is Persian. I swear she cut clumps out of his coat to make it look as if he had mange. He's as healthy as I am, but she's so…so *single* she scares me."

She patted his shoulder consolingly, grinning at Amanda.

He rubbed a hand over his eyes, then looked into hers with curiosity. "I heard about you finding a baby in here. What happened? Luke said it was sick."

"Actually, he's only teething," Shelly replied, placing utensils and a small bowl of butter cubes in front of him.

"And you're keeping him?"

"Just until Pine Run sends a caseworker." She felt a certain satisfaction, though, knowing she'd opened an account for Max this morning at the savings and loan. Whatever happened to him, he'd eventually have money for an education.

"So…where is he?"

"At home with Connor."

She knew that was a mistake the moment the words were out of her mouth.

He raised an eyebrow and glanced at Amanda. "Connor?"

Amanda came to lean on the counter beside him. She was a column of elegance today in mossy green. "The new pediatrician at the medical clinic. Ask me what he's doing at her house?"

Jack was suddenly far more interested in Shelly's life than his own. "What's he doing at Shelly's house?"

"Helping with the baby," Amanda replied with a grin at Shelly. "At least, that's supposed to be the plan. And the plan was supposed to include only one night, but so far it's stretched to two, and he kissed her yesterday in front of God and everybody, and seems to be sleeping in with the baby this morning, so..."

Shelly reached behind her for the tall paper cup of mocha she'd been about to add whipped cream to when Jack rushed in. She did that now, put a lid on it and a paper heat collar, then handed it to Amanda.

"You can go now," Shelly said with a frown for her friend.

Amanda smiled. "But it's so interesting here."

Shelly smiled back. "It'll be even more interesting when we have to call an ambulance for you. 'Bye!"

Amanda heaved a theatrical sigh. "To think that

you used to want my opinion on things. Then Connor came along and I'm cast off like an old worn-out high-top.''

''Amanda,'' Shelly threatened, ''if you don't stop…''

Amanda headed for the door with a smile for Shelly over her shoulder. ''See you. Let me know if you need Dr. Spock's book, or maybe one on how to get along with a man.'' She pulled the door open, then turned to add for Jack, ''Get some backbone, Hartman. Tell Paula and Mary Kay they're not your type.''

He smiled flatly at her. ''Don't let us keep you, Amanda.''

She waved and closed the door behind her.

Jack turned to Shelly. ''So the new doc's caught your fancy?''

''I don't have a fancy,'' she replied, ''and if I did, it would be fleet of foot. What would you do if I wasn't here every morning to see that you have your morning pastry?''

He cut a neat square of pasty off with his fork. ''Would falling in love mean you couldn't still run the restaurant? I mean, it's not like being a priest who doesn't have a family so he can devote himself completely to God and his job. It's just a restaurant.''

She knew he'd meant no offense, but she saw him think twice about that last remark. ''Not that it's *just* a restaurant. I mean, the whole town knows if you don't hear the gossip here, it isn't true. And if you're missing any piece of information about the town or anyone in it, you'll find it here. But you do get to have a life, Shelly.''

She nodded and topped up his coffee. ''I know. I guess it's just that…if I had a life, I'm not sure what I'd do with it.''

He grinned, his Danish half disposed of while she'd been talking. ''We're millionaires. The world's full of opportunities we didn't have before.''

''Yes. I guess I don't know where to start. I want to do things for the town, I want to do things for the coffee shop, for my house, for me.'' She leaned back against an empty length of work counter and narrowed her focus on him. ''What are *you* going to do with your fortune?''

He shrugged. ''Beats me. I'm waiting for inspiration to strike.''

''Then why are you harassing me?'' she asked, swatting his arm with the towel she held.

''Habit,'' he replied.

She made a face at him. ''I saw the now-famous 'wolf,''' Shelly said. ''And I think it's a dog.''

''Well, why didn't you catch him for me? He keeps running away from me.''

''Who wouldn't?''

Dan called from the kitchen. ''Telephone, Shelly!''

''You'd better leave me a big tip,'' Shelly told Jack as she went into the kitchen to take the call.

''After that crack?'' he shouted after her. ''I don't think so!''

It was Luke.

"Caseworker's on her way," he said.

Shelly felt a sudden, urgent rush of emotion. She saw Max's little face in her mind's eye, felt his warm body on her shoulder, even heard his screams that could go on forever, and thought desperately that she didn't want to lose him.

"Have you found the mother?" she asked.

"No," he answered. "Not even a clue so far."

"Do you think…" She hesitated, almost afraid to form the thought, to say it aloud. She cleared her throat and rushed the words out. "Do you think they'd let me keep him until you do?"

"Well…I don't think so, Shelly. I mean, if you were a relative, they might. But to be a foster home, you have to have interviews, inspections of your home, background checks. They have to be careful about…"

"Of course." She didn't know what she was thinking. They didn't know her from Adam, and wouldn't just arbitrarily place an abandoned baby in her care.

"Where is Max?" Luke asked.

"He's home with Connor right now," she replied, "but why don't you bring the caseworker to the medical center. I don't want her to think we were careless with him."

"Why would she think that?"

"Oh, you know. Single woman, single man—even though he is a doctor—sharing a household purportedly for the sake of the baby. It sounds iffy even to me, and I know it isn't."

"Whatever you say. She's expected to be here by noon."

"Okay. I'll call Connor."

CONNOR WASN'T ENTIRELY surprised by how upset Shelly seemed that the caseworker was finally coming to relieve her of the baby. She'd grown a little more comfortable with Max and less fearful of her own inability to cope. No one knew better than he did how affection for a child could change your life.

He'd met her with Max at the medical center as she'd asked and now watched her pace with the baby as they waited for Luke to appear with the caseworker. Max, who'd been awake much of the morning, now lolled against her shoulder, his little fingers entwined in her hair.

Nathan Perkins appeared in the doorway. Though only thirty-six, he was prematurely gray with a paternal air that contributed to the confidence he inspired in his patients. While waiting for Shelly, Connor had explained her attachment to the boy over the brief time they'd cared for him. Nathan studied her in concern.

"They look right together," he said quietly to Connor. "Seems a shame to take him away from her to put him in a foster home."

"I was thinking the same thing."

A tinkling bell over the door to the clinic sent Nathan to the waiting room. There was the sound of cordial greetings, then footsteps returning to the examining room.

Shelly stopped pacing and turned to Connor, her eyes dark with sadness.

He felt as though he'd been stabbed.

Luke, with a forced smile, introduced Shelly and Connor to Louise Pearson. She was a no-nonsense-looking woman probably in her fifties with gray hair in a bun and an air of experience. She smiled fractionally as Shelly offered her hand.

"I'm so sorry it took this long to get here," the woman said briskly. "Our office is a disaster at the moment, and the weather and the erratic phone service haven't helped any. It was kind of you to do our job for us, Miss Dupree."

"I was happy to, Mrs. Pearson. He's a very sweet little boy." Shelly bounced a frantic glance off Connor, then said quickly, "In fact, I asked the sheriff about the possibility of caring for Max until his mother is found."

The woman gave her that almost-smile. "I'm sorry, but unless you're a family member, we can't do that. Max has to go to a foster home where we've screened the parents."

"It's just that Max has a little bit of a fever," Connor put in quickly, touching a hand to the baby's face. Thanks to the on-again, off-again effects of teething, Max looked flushed at the moment and was rubbing his eyes and beginning to cry peevishly. "Dr. Perkins and I thought it might be a good idea if Max stayed here for a few days where he'd have some continuity of care. I mean, if he's just going to go into foster care anyway.''

"Oh.'' The woman put her own hand to the baby's pink cheek. Max whined dutifully and began to cry. "I didn't realize he was ill.''

Shelly began to bounce the baby on her shoulder and walk around the office with him. Connor handed her a small plastic bag with the frozen pacifier inside.

Max took it into his mouth and quieted, leaning into Shelly's neck and fisting his hand in her hair.

"Is it just teething?'' Mrs. Pearson asked Connor.

"It's the complications of teething,'' Connor replied, hoping she'd go for it. "Fever, irritable stomach, sleeplessness.''

She looked uncertain about whether or not that was sufficient reason to leave him when Nathan weighed in with "Nothing serious at this point, Louise, but Shelly and Connor have learned how to keep him comfortable and that's important to a baby. And where Max might be disruptive to one of your foster homes, Shelly has nothing else to worry about.''

Louise Pearson was nobody's fool. She studied Shelly as she paced back toward her, Max dutifully closing heavy eyelids. "You're one of the Main Street Millionaires, aren't you?'' she asked. "You have a restaurant.''

Shelly nodded. "Max loves it there. All the patrons fuss over him.''

"And when he's not there,'' Connor added, "he's here at the clinic with me.''

Nathan put an arm around Connor's shoulder. "I can vouch for their characters, Louise," he said. "Connor and I went to medical school together and I invited him here to join me in the clinic. That has to tell you how much I value him as a human being and a doctor. And I've known Shelly forever. She's kind and honest and responsible."

Mrs. Pearson looked from one to the other, clearly a woman who wasn't easily swayed. She turned to Luke. "And what's your opinion of all this?"

Luke turned his hat in his hands. "I'm the one who suggested Shelly take care of the baby the night she found him and we couldn't get through to your office. The doc volunteered to help her."

That was a little shy of the truth, but no one was going to correct him.

The woman finally gave them a brief, serious nod. "All right. I'll leave him with you, but I'm going to check with you daily on how he's doing, and the moment he's free of fever, I have to take him."

Shelly nodded with the same gravity, but the moment Mrs. Pearson started for the door, Shelly turned to Connor with a blinding smile. "Thank you," she mouthed.

Luke and Nathan followed the caseworker out of the room.

Shelly breathed a deep sigh of relief. "I know I can't keep him forever," she said quietly, "but I felt as though I couldn't let him go yet." Her expression grew serious again. "Why should he go to strangers when he seems to be adjusting to me?'' She looked into Connor's eyes and corrected on an even lower note, ''To us.''

He considered that a significant moment. She felt allied to him, connected through the baby. The situation couldn't last forever so he was going to have to make the best of it.

''Since you haven't found a place to stay yet,'' she suggested, ''why don't you just stay with me for the week? That is if you want to continue to help with Max.''

''Sure,'' he replied easily, as though that suggestion hadn't played right into his hands. ''I appreciate that.''

''Okay.'' Max was now asleep on her shoulder and she tossed her hair with a new confidence. ''I'll take Max back to the coffee shop with me so you can enjoy the rest of your day off.''

She turned to leave and found Nathan standing in the doorway. ''Thank you,'' she said, wrapping an arm around him and kissing his cheek.

''Happy to help,'' he said, touching the baby's head. ''This baby deserves you.''

He walked her to the front door and opened it for her, Connor following behind.

''Come to the Cup for dinner!'' she called back to Connor.

''I will,'' he promised.

Connor and Nathan stood in the doorway together, watching her walk away.

''Good woman,'' Nathan said.

"Yeah," Connor replied.

"She could restore a man's faith in womankind."

"Yeah."

Nathan fixed him with a speaking glance. "You're going to take advantage of this opportunity, aren't you?"

Connor didn't take his eyes off her until she rounded the corner and was out of sight. He confirmed quietly but emphatically, "Oh, yeah."

Chapter Six

Over the weekend, Shelly began to feel as though she really had a life. She, Connor and Max were a cohesive unit navigating the tricky waters of busy schedules and the needs of a baby. Shelly wondered if Louise Pearson would change her mind about letting them care for the baby if she could see the hoops they had to leap through to meet the demands of their work and still see that the baby was sheltered and cared for at all times. They were like a *20/20* segment on the modern family.

Shelly could not remember being happier. On Friday afternoon Max played and slept in a playpen Nathan's wife, Vickie, had brought over that afternoon and helped Shelly set up in the far corner behind the counter. Everyone stopped to coo at him, make faces, talk baby talk. He smiled and laughed all the time.

The news media was still around, looking for leads on Max's mother. Shelly was torn between wanting them to find her and hoping the woman was long gone. In any case, they were good for business and she was as courteous and accommodating to them as she was to everyone who visited The Brimming Cup. Though she did serve Harvey Brinkman cold coffee and managed to forget the condiments on his ham and cheese sandwich.

Connor walked in shortly after six. Shelly was stunned by how handsome he was in a distressed leather jacket over a black turtleneck and slacks. She was busy taking an order but waved at him. While Shelly jotted down the details on how Dean and Finn wanted their steaks prepared, she heard Max's squeal of delight as Connor went to the playpen and lifted him out.

As she went back to the kitchen with the order, she pointed Connor to an empty booth in the back.

Dean, however, invited Connor and Max to join him and Finn.

"I'd like to," Connor said, "but he might get fussy and ruin your nice, quiet dinner."

"Nah," Dean denied, moving farther into the booth and patting the table beside him. "Finn, here, has raised a whole passel of kids, and I've never had my own, but love to admire everybody else's. Besides, I've got this crick in my neck I want to talk to you about."

Though Shelly was busy, she noticed that they seemed to get on well and that Max entertained himself with a spoon while the men talked and ate. He didn't turn rowdy until they'd finished eating and he discovered he could bang the spoon on the table or the crockery for a cacophonous effect.

She saw Connor put on his jacket and slide out of the booth with Max on his hip.

"Pleasure to meet you, Doc." Dean's booming voice carried across the restaurant to the counter where Shelly was serving up coconut cream pie. "Hope to get to visit with you again."

"Likewise, Mr. Kenning," Connor replied, "Mr. Hollis."

He came toward the counter, his attention snagged by the pie to which she was adding a decorative dollop of whipped cream.

"Yum," he said. "Can you bring some of that home?"

She cut another piece and placed it in a take-out box. "It'll be another few hours before I get there. Can you carry this and Max, too?"

"No problem," he said with an appreciative grin. "Thank you. And your chicken strips are superior. No wonder your customers like them. If you get me Max's snowsuit, I'll take him home with me."

"It's in the back. Hold on a minute and I'll get it for you."

She delivered the first slice of pie then ran into the kitchen where Dan was working like a particularly brilliant machine, the grill covered with burgers, steaks, cottage fries.

"Everything okay?" she asked as she ran to her

small office, retrieved the suit and ran back toward the front.

"Everything's always okay," he replied without turning to her. That was always his answer.

She passed the suit over the counter to Connor, then spotted Dean, holding up his coffee cup. She grabbed the pot and headed for his booth.

When she returned, Connor had Max's legs in the suit and was working on his flailing arms. She replaced the pot, then hurried to help him, bumping noses with the baby to distract him while Connor got his arms in the suit. Then Connor stood him up on a stool and held his hands out as Shelly drew up the zipper. She pulled his hood up and tied it in place while the baby laughed.

"I'll be home around ten," she said, walking them to the door.

"Call me when you leave and I'll put the coffee on," he said, then arched an eyebrow in question. "Or is that even appealing when you serve it all day?"

She leaned toward him conspiratorially. "I use basic good stuff here, but I have really good stuff at home. Do put the coffee on."

"All right. See you then."

And then as naturally as though they'd been dressing babies and parting at the door of the restaurant for years, he leaned down to kiss her and she stretched up to meet his mouth.

The instant their lips touched, she remembered that it wasn't natural for them at all, but her mouth didn't seem to care. It was a tender kiss, a simple meeting of uncomplicated feelings of affection and connection.

But it still hit her like a hammer.

She closed the coffee-shop door behind her, her lips tickling, her senses reeling.

It was after ten before she prepared the deposit, put it in the safe, then remembered to call Connor and tell him she was on her way. She locked up the shop and headed along the street.

Connor was standing on the porch when she reached the house.

"What are you doing out here?" she asked as she climbed the steps.

"Watching you," he replied, pushing the front door open for her. "That's a long, dark block."

"Thank you," she said, "but Jester's safe."

"Jester's now full of people who don't usually live here," he reminded her. "Max is asleep. Time for the Midnight Marauders to frolic."

She went to the carrier where Max slept and felt a rush of emotion at his look of complete contentment. His tiny fingers were splayed in response to some happy dream where he smiled, then snuggled even deeper into the blankets.

She caught the carrier in one hand and took it with her as they walked into the kitchen. "Midnight Marauders?" she asked, placing the carrier on a seldom-used corner of the counter.

"Us." He laughed. "One of my patients in L.A. was part of a family with four children under seven, and that's what the father and mother called themselves. When there's a baby or children around, your day is so focused on them you're hardly aware of your own needs. When they're asleep you finally come alive and feel as though you want to take over the landscape because the world is now yours again.''

She pulled her coat off and went to the cupboard for plates as he poured coffee. She gave the cupboard her customary yank and almost flew across the room when it gave immediately.

''Careful.'' Connor came to steady her. ''I fixed that,'' he explained. ''And watch the drawer, too. The runners needed a little soap.''

''They were dirty?'' she asked in surprise.

He studied her a moment, apparently wondering if she was serious. Then seeing that she was, he laughed lightly, caught her arm and pushed her into a chair. ''No, the soap was to help it slide. I also tightened the wobbly towel rack in the bathroom down here, and the light switch now works on the back porch. Sit there and I'll wait on you.''

''That was unnecessary, but very appreciated.'' She watched him work at the counter and admired his broad back and long legs in the snug jeans with a sort of wistful budding of lust she knew she couldn't indulge. ''You found my father's tools.''

''Yeah. Mine are still in storage. He had a great shop. I'd kill for his ShopMan.''

''Is that the big table saw thing?''

''I've wanted one for ages, but haven't had enough

time or space to put one to good use. Maybe I'll be able to find it in Jester.''

He brought two steaming mugs of coffee to the table, then the pie she'd sent home with him divided onto two plates.

''You're pretty good at this,'' she observed, the weariness she'd felt when she closed the restaurant suddenly replaced by a sharp awareness of her surroundings. ''We could use you at the Cup on weekends.''

He looked up from dipping his fork into the pie. ''Do I get to keep my tips?''

She was sure those smiling good looks would earn them. ''We put them in a pot and the waitress splits her take with Dan.''

''Sounds fair. But I think if I had to carry more than two plates, there'd be some serious loss of dinnerware and product. Besides...'' He took a bite of pie, rolled his eyes, then chewed and swallowed. ''Your customers would miss your personal service. Dean and Henry talked at great length about what a great girl you are.'' He smiled apologetically. ''*Girl* being their term, not mine. And how you've made a seamless transition from the restaurant your parents ran to the Cup as it is now.''

She sighed with satisfaction. It had been a good day. And it was nice to hear that her efforts in the coffee shop kept her regulars happy.

''Jester is full of great people. Did Dean say what he's going to do with his money?''

"He has an investment plan that's worthy of Wall Street, and he said something about taking a cruise if he can get Delilah Burke to go with him. Who's Delilah Burke?"

"Well, that's promising!" she exclaimed. "I think he's been sweet on her since they were in high school together. But she married someone else, moved to Helena, and come home to Pine Run after he died. Dean never married. But it's been clear since she got back that he'd like to…you know…rekindle the romance."

"It gives you faith in love," he said, "when even people in their late sixties are doing it."

She sipped at her coffee. "Had you lost faith in it?"

"It wasn't lost but seriously dented." He grinned at her. "But you've been a sort of emotional rubber mallet."

"Um…" She narrowed one eye, trying to imagine if such a comparison was good or bad.

"Okay, pitiful metaphor. I mean the dent is gone. I feel as though my feelings about love have been reshaped, reformed."

She was flattered. Even…touched. But she was determined to resist his charms. He was too unsettling, and she was a woman with roots that ran deep.

She pushed her plate away and leaned toward him on her forearms. "We're here together for Max. You keep forgetting that."

He shook his head, apparently unaffected by her attempt to thwart him. "I'm not forgetting anything.

You're just denying what's right in front of your face.''

"What's in front of my face is a legacy that I'm required to uphold and maintain. And, finally, opportunities to...be free.''

He frowned at that. "Now that doesn't make sense. Are you determined to keep the Cup going as a tribute to your parents, or are you straining at the bit to take advantage of your winnings and be free? And whichever it is, why did you want so desperately to keep Max if your life is either about the pressure of work, or the possibilities of freedom? In either case, he doesn't fit. Nothing fits.''

"He was abandoned! He needed me!''

"He needed someone. Mrs. Pearson probably had a perfectly suitable home for him to go to. I think *you* need Max. When he dropped into your life, you finally realized that you want children, though apparently you've been telling yourself since you inherited the restaurant that you don't have time for them. You want a family. You want the day-to-day demands of loving and being loved just like everyone else. Why do you pretend you don't?''

"I want...'' she began firmly, then had difficulty finishing the sentence. What did she want? At the moment she hadn't a clue, except she'd thought that this was nice—having someone to come home to on weekend nights when everyone else was gathering at the Heartbreaker, or with their families. Someone who stood on the porch and watched protectively as she walked home.

That is—it was nice until he began interrogating her.

"I want," she started again more quietly, "for you to stop *telling* me what I want. I'm here because it was what the Duprees did and I've adjusted. I've more than adjusted—I've settled in. So don't...rock the boat."

He went to the counter for the pot and topped up their cups. "Don't make you think about it, you mean?" he asked when he came back to the table.

She ignored him and forked her last bite of pie.

"What did you want to do," he asked gently, "that you didn't get to do because of The Brimming Cup?"

She sighed and sat back. "Almost everything," she admitted for the first time, even to herself. "I wanted to play with the other kids instead of doing dishes and setting tables. I wanted to go to the movies with my friends instead of waitressing Friday and Saturday nights because the young woman who waited tables for us had a boyfriend and didn't want to work week-end nights. Then as a young woman I wanted to explore the possibilities of a liberal arts education, but it was clear that my mother's health was weakening and my father was going to need me even more. I got to go to culinary school, but came right back to help out."

He pushed his cup aside and put a hand on hers across the small table. "Why do you feel guilty about wanting something else? You're entitled to the life you want. Particularly now that you have the opportunity to get it for yourself.''

She frowned at him. ''There you go again. Do you want me here, or not?''

He met her eyes and held them. ''I guess that depends on whether you want to be here or not.''

''Because your life's already been...*dented* by someone who didn't want the same thing you wanted and you don't want that to happen again?''

Was that the root of his concern? he wondered as he looked into her troubled eyes. Not that she might miss life's possibilities, but that he had to know which direction she was heading so he could decide whether or not to become further involved? Was he thinking that if she was going to live for the restaurant, or take off in search of herself, the crush was off?

He wasn't sure. The moment was too tumultuous to tell. His visions of his own life—wife, children, big dog, barbecues, trips to the zoo—were all entangled in Shelly's guilt-ridden but legitimate sadness over a lost childhood. She had a right to life the way she wanted it now that she could finally do something about it.

''Maybe,'' he admitted on a sigh.

She stared back at him one surprised moment then seemed to lose her head of steam. ''Well, go ahead and ruin the argument for me by being honest,'' she chided with a very small smile.

Max chose that moment to wake up and scream for attention.

Connor pushed his chair back, intending to go get him.

Shelly stopped him with a raised hand. "I'll take him up with me."

"You just came home from work," he objected.

"I know," she said reasonably, "but if you weren't here, I'd have to deal with him."

"But that's *why* I'm here."

"No, you're not. You're here to help me when he's sick, not just when he's crying. Every single mother in the world has to cope with a baby who needs her whether or not she's rested. And it's just temporary. Next week, when he goes back to Pine Run, I'll get all the rest I need."

She put Max to her shoulder in what was now a very graceful and comfortable movement, took a bottle out of the refrigerator one-handed, heated it, then went toward the stairs. "Good night," she called over her shoulder as Max, recognizing the bottle, made happy noises and reached toward it, little fingers outspread.

Connor put the dishes in the dishwasher, locked up, turned out the lights, then climbed into his lonely bed. Only it wasn't lonely for long. Sean Connery, apparently fed up with the noise and disturbance from his mistress's new pet, leaped onto the bed and curled up in the hollow between Connor's chin and shoulder.

He was purring so loudly, Connor didn't think he'd be able to sleep.

He was right. But it wasn't just the cat that kept him awake. He could hear everything going on upstairs. Max was up every hour or so. Connor heard his unhappy cries, their gradual abatement as Shelly walked the floor or spoke to him in a gentle tone. There would be quiet for some time, then it would all erupt again and he would hear her pacing the floor. She'd been down once for the teething stick in the freezer, but it wasn't effective tonight.

The scenario had repeated itself for a fourth time when he glanced at the clock, having to pat down the fluffy cat's coat to be able to read it. Three twenty-seven.

He threw the covers off and swung his feet to the floor. Sean Connery meowed peevishly but didn't move.

He ran up the stairs to find Shelly with the crying baby in one arm, reaching to the foot of the bed for her robe with the other. She looked like a zombie replacement for the real Shelly. She was pale, her eyes red rimmed and bloodshot, her hair rumpled.

He took the baby from her, holding off her interfering hands with his free one.

"I'm doing this!" she shouted at him, tossing the robe down angrily. She was exhausted and grumpy.

Max screamed at her raised voice.

"You're upsetting the baby," Connor said, certain that would guilt her into letting him help.

"If you weren't here..." She began the argument she'd used earlier.

"I *am* here," he interrupted firmly. "And let's not analyze why right now, okay? Let's just get through tonight."

He sat on the side of the bed that showed the least disturbance, and held Max against him. The bedclothes, he noticed, smelled of lilacs. Almost instantly, the baby's cries changed from angry screams to simple complaint.

"I *hate* that you can do that with him," she said, folding her arms. He did his best to ignore the small protrusion of nipples through her nightshirt.

"When a baby needs comfort, a mother's soft, gentle arms are just the right thing," he said, patting the mattress beside him. "But when he hurts and doesn't know why and everything in his confusing little world seems to be attacking him, he needs to feel muscle, power, protection."

"But you can't protect him from sore gums any more than I can."

"It's an illusion." He smiled, patting the mattress again. "Come back to bed. He knows he has a champion, so he'll feel more secure and get over it himself. Lie down," he prompted again. "It can work for you, too."

She didn't move, studying him suspiciously.

He rolled his eyes. "I haven't gotten any more sleep than you have. I don't have the energy to seduce you.

And frankly,'' he smiled apologetically, ''you're not at your seductive best at the moment.''

She looked from the bed to him, apparently unable to choose between her annoyance with him and the inviting aspect of climbing into the covers again.

The baby stopped crying. She opened her mouth to speak, but Connor put a finger to his lips, a suggestion that they do nothing to disturb Max's tenuous hold on sleep.

Marching to the doorway with a tantalizing sway of her hips, she flipped off the light then stomped back to her side of the bed and climbed in. It was only a double bed, and she stayed well on her side.

Connor closed his eyes, finding her even more exhausting than the baby.

Chapter Seven

Shelly dreamed of warmth and blissful quiet. She was cocooned in soft blankets that were slightly scratchy but wonderfully comfortable. She was aware of her mind and body drifting up to wakefulness and fought it by clutching the blankets to her and trying to hold on to the quiet.

She moved a foot, rubbing against her mattress in an attempt to widen her stance and resist the encroaching light of day. In a move that startled her out of sleep despite her efforts to hold on to it, the mattress on which she lay rubbed her in return.

She raised her head, completely disoriented. Through the hair over her face, she saw that she lay atop a gray T-shirt with the letters *UCLA* on the front. She swiped the hair out of her eyes and raised them to discover that inside the shirt was a man. Connor. Not the smiling, argumentative, usually nonthreatening Connor she was used to seeing in a lab coat or the jeans and sweatshirt he wore around the house.

This was Connor with not much of anything on,

except the T-shirt and, she hoped, the boxer shorts he usually wore to bed. She didn't want to make a point of looking to be sure. She could feel the mild rasp of his legs against her smooth ones.

Warmth flooded her face—and every part of her body in contact with his. She pushed herself up to sit back on her heels, then realized she was straddling his leg. She scrambled onto the other side of him. Sean Connery, she noticed for the first time, lay on the other pillow.

She saw Connor's turbulent eyes note her heightened awareness as they ran over her, feature by feature.

"Where's the baby?" she asked in sudden alarm.

He pointed to the carrier on the floor beside the bed. She had to lean over him to see. Max was fast asleep, dark lashes resting quietly on plump cheeks, tiny mouth open.

"When you snuggled in," Connor said, his voice quiet but as rich and deep as his eyes, "I put him back in the carrier."

She slipped back onto her knees on his other side and frowned in consternation. "I'm sorry. I can't believe I did that. I'm usually so aware of him when I have him in bed with me. I never roll on him or..."

He put a hand to her hair, running his fingers through it to comb it back from her face. "It's all right. You knew I had him, so you relaxed."

He looked anything but relaxed, though he lay quietly, and she felt no urgency in his touch. "Did you get any sleep?"

A small but very wicked smile curved his lips. "Not much, no."

She would have felt guilty, but he didn't seem at all distressed by the cause of his insomnia.

"I'm sorry," she whispered.

"Don't be," he replied, still wearing that smile. "Just kiss me and tell me there'll be more nights like this in my future." A small laugh escaped him. "Well, not precisely like this, but with you sprawled over me, exhausted by our lovemaking."

She was suddenly trapped by a vision of that scenario. After lying in his arms the past few hours of the night she *felt* different, as though what he wanted out of their relationship had somehow seeped into her. She imagined what would happen if she leaned into him now and kissed him.

But the dim light coming in through the window suddenly jarred her into reality. It must be well after six! For the first time in years—literally—she'd be late opening the restaurant.

She scrambled out of bed, thinking, *What am I doing? This lolling in bed with a man I've known only a few days isn't for me! I'm a hardworking, sensible woman.* She turned in a circle, having completely lost her bearings though this was the room she'd slept in every one of her twenty-eight years.

"I have a business to run! Trips to take! A baby to

care for! And, yes, those goals are not at all compatible, but I'm stressed, all right!''

She didn't realize she'd said those words aloud until Connor, still lying in bed, said with an amused frown, ''What are you stressed about? You're the one who slept.''

She snatched a white cross-training, full-arch-support shoe off the floor and pointed it at him. ''Don't be clever, okay? I'm an hour late opening the Cup, thanks to you. If you were wide-awake all that time, why didn't you wake *me?*''

His shrug suggested that the big hunk of male lying in her bed had been helpless to do that. ''Had I awakened you,'' he said, his voice lowering an octave, ''it wouldn't have been to send you off to work.''

Warmth flooded her face again and she had to storm off to the bathroom as the image of their lovemaking filled her head again. She could resist him only if he was unaware of how much she wanted him.

DAN, BLESS HIM, HAD OPENED the coffee shop on time.

''It's all right,'' he said, taking the baby carrier from her and following her into her office as she thanked him profusely. ''It's been slow. But what happened?''

She looked into his face, preparing a fib about the baby, but he smiled suddenly and said, ''Oh.''

''What, 'Oh'?'' she asked irritably, ripping a clean apron out of her closet and putting it on. ''The baby was up most of the night, and therefore, so was I." It was partially true.

He pointed to the baby, fast asleep in his carrier. He'd hardly even stirred while she'd dressed him over Connor's suggestion that she leave Max with him. But she'd been determined to lean on him less, depend more upon her own abilities. She had them. At least, she used to have them. She'd once functioned fine on her own. She'd longed for a man, for children, for family, but when they hadn't seemed to be on her horizon, she'd managed on her own. She was not going to lose her ability to do that.

"He's sleeping now," she said pointedly, "because he kept me up all night. That's why I'm late. Not, 'Oh.' And don't think I don't know what you meant by that."

She put the baby in the playpen in the corner near the counter and wiped off a table, then set it up again. Then she got a large piece of poster board from the supply closet and sat on a stool at the counter with a handful of felt-tip pens.

With no customers in the shop, Dan stayed behind the counter and poured himself a cup of coffee.

"I meant," he said, coming to stand in front of her, "that I thought you looked a little—" she glanced up and he paused to consider the word carefully "—rumpled," he finally said.

She leaned around him to look at her reflection in the pie case. Her hair was smooth, her makeup minimal but neat, her apron clean.

"Not that kind of rumpled," he said, fixing her with a paternal look. "Your…your personal tidiness is rumpled. For once you look as though you *don't* have all your ducks in a row. You're doubting the world as you've come to know it." He leaned on the counter and toasted her with his cup. "That's a sign of maturity."

She took issue with that. "That's a sign of sloppiness."

He shook his head patiently. "No. If we're lucky as children, we grow up wanting to emulate the life we had as children. It isn't until we grow and learn and experience other things that we realize we can build on what we knew, but we have the right, even the responsibility, to be who we are."

She extended both arms to encompass The Brimming Cup. "This is who I am," she said.

He looked into her eyes the way her father sometimes used to. He often saw in her things her mother missed because Alice Dupree was so busy being his support system.

Dan nodded. "I know that was once true," he said gently. "But do you think it still is?"

Dean, Finn and Henry walked in and Dan quickly retreated to the kitchen. The place was suddenly filled with their banter and their laughter. They all looked into Max's carrier and, seeing that he was asleep, went quietly to their back booth.

Shelly poured their coffee, took their orders, then sat down again with her poster board project.

"What're you doing?" Jack Hartman walked in and stopped to peer over her shoulder.

"Making a list of possible projects to tackle in town."

"Tackle?" He walked around the counter and poured his own coffee.

"With money," she replied. "I'm taking a poll of my customers to see what they'd like done first. I want to help with a few things."

"And how much have you earmarked for this bountiful work?" He sat beside her and watched her print with the squeaky pens.

"Not sure," she replied. "I guess it depends on what has to be done. What do you think should be first? Cleaning up Catherine and Jester's statue? The church roof? New equipment for the school playground?" She put all those things on her list, then stopped to think, the top of a marker against her chin. "The town hall needs a new lawn. It was brown all summer."

Jack sighed. "I'd like to see Catherine's statue cleaned," he said, his expression suddenly grim, "only if I won't be around to have to look at it."

Shelly remembered belatedly that Catherine had been Jack's dead wife's ancestor, and when Caroline, his wife, had been alive, everyone used to remark on how much she looked like her. She knew that the statue was always a painful reminder for Jack.

"The park needs work, too," she said, hoping to distract him. She hated it when he talked about leaving

Jester. He was a devoted and conscientious veterinarian, and a good friend.

"And the bleachers on the baseball field," he said, shrugging off the grim mood and getting into the spirit of her project. "There are more termites than people in them during the summer."

"Order up, Shelly!" Dan called.

Shelly handed Jack her pen and slid off the stool to pick up her orders. "I'd like to get a list of ten things that need work," she said. "You're welcome to add your thoughts."

"What's going on up there?" Dean asked as Shelly put his bacon and eggs in front of him.

She explained about her project as she served Finn his French toast, and Henry a waffle with a side of sausage. "You guys have any ideas?"

"A public rest room downtown," Dean said.

"Now, that's a good idea."

"Clean up Catherine's statue," Henry added.

Shelly nodded. "Already got that one. I'd appreciate it if you gentlemen would check out the list before you leave and tell me which project should have priority."

"Flower baskets hanging from the street signs," Finn contributed. "We used to do that in better times. It doesn't take all that much money and it looks pretty when visitors come. It also used to cheer me up."

"Flowers are good," Shelly concurred. "I'll add that to the list."

Luke walked in, followed by several people who

worked in the Town Hall, and Shelly became too busy to think about anything but food. As she hurried past with orders, she asked Jack to add Dean's and his cronies' suggestions.

The growing list attracted more attention and more opinions. Jack made a grid numbered from one to ten at the right of each improvement suggested, and when he left, he posted it for her near the door so that customers could check a particular item's number of importance before they left. She noted that across the top, he'd printed, "Shelly's Projects."

She was wiping off a table later, folding up a *Plain Talker* someone had left and saw with annoyance that she'd made the front page again, along with Dean and the Perkinses. It was simply three separate photos of them with captions under the headline, Keeping Up With The Main Street Millionaires.

She was shocked to read that the caption under her photo said she'd opened an account for the baby. How did Brinkman know that?

She wanted to scream. Instead, she called the publisher of the paper and asked for Harvey's head wrapped in the next edition.

CONNOR DELIVERED A BABY. The terrified husband had driven his wife to the medical center rather than risk the icy drive to the hospital in Pine Run. He was a large man in a complete panic. He did not want to assist with the delivery and chose to stay in the waiting room with his three boys.

But his wife, who assured Connor that she was fine and everything seemed to be progressing just right, barely had time to climb onto the table before she delivered.

He held up the pink little girl for her to see.

She stared at it in disbelief and demanded, "Where did you get her?"

He analyzed that question from every angle and still couldn't decide how to answer. He finally settled for "Pardon me?"

"It's a girl!" she said, reaching for her, her face suddenly wreathed in smiles. "We have three boys. I thought boys was all I'd ever have. But it's a girl!"

"Didn't you have an ultrasound?"

"Yes, but we wanted to be surprised about the sex. And...I am!" She clutched his hand. "You're good luck, Doc. All Nathan ever handed me were boys."

"I'll ask for a raise," Connor laughed. "Let me do a few tests here, then you can have her right back and see your family."

The father wrapped his arms around Connor, but the boys, about six, seven and eight, looked at him as though he'd betrayed them.

"You'll like her," he promised. "When she gets older, she'll have girlfriends right about the time you're wanting to go out on dates and having trouble meeting girls. It'll make your lives a lot easier."

The oldest one, Albie, looked doubtful. "Maybe I won't want to meet girls. Maybe I'm going into space."

"Guys always want to meet girls," Connor assured him. "Even in space."

"I want to meet Spider-Man."

"Well...*he's* got a girlfriend."

Albie looked suspicious. "You're sure?"

"Absolutely."

Then an older man with difficulty breathing was brought in by his daughter and granddaughter and Connor had to devote his attention to determining the problem. He was relieved to discover some time later that it was simply an empty inhaler.

The office was quiet by midafternoon when Nathan arrived to do some paperwork. Connor sat in his office, making a list of supplies that were running low.

"I can't tell you how great it is to have you here!" Nathan said, handing Connor a cup of coffee and a small paper bag containing two large cookies. When Connor moved to vacate the chair behind the desk, Nathan raised a hand to make him stay. He took a chair that faced the desk. "Used to be that I had to do this paperwork at night after I closed the office. There was never time in the middle of the afternoon."

Connor made a sound of approval. "Ooh. Cookies from the bookstore. Where does Amanda Bradley get them?"

"From Gwen Tanner, who runs the boardinghouse and caters on the side. Apparently she doesn't know what to do with her money, either, because she's still baking."

"Thank goodness." Connor bit into the cookie.

"I'm glad to be here. I delivered a baby this morning, mother and daughter doing fine. Said to tell you they like me better than you because all you've ever delivered are boys. I gave them a girl."

Nathan laughed. "The Carbys? Francie must have been in shock."

"She couldn't stop smiling. The boys weren't too pleased, though."

"They'll learn to love her. It might take seventeen or eighteen years. How's Max?"

"Thriving."

"And Shelly?"

"She's catching on. Getting possessive about him. That child's going to have so much sensory stimulation from being in the coffee shop that he'll be ahead of all the other babies when he...when he goes into foster care."

"Maybe Luke will find his mother."

"If he does, will she want him back? She got rid of him once."

While Nathan mulled that over, Connor added with a sigh, "Whatever happens, Shelly's going to be upset when Mrs. Pearson takes him away."

"Yeah. Maybe it'll encourage her to get serious about you." Nathan grinned at him. "You are doing all in your power to bring that about?"

Connor sipped at his paper cup of coffee and gave Nathan a self-deprecating look over the rim. "She's remarkably resistant to my charms."

"Some women don't appreciate subtlety."

Connor had to laugh. "I have not been subtle. What she fails to appreciate is honesty."

Nathan shrugged. "Maybe that's the wrong approach. She's won the lottery and a baby was dropped into her lap. Maybe what she needs from you is a sort of phantom lover—a step into fantasy. Then, eventually, when Louise has to take the baby away, and she has to do something settled and sensible with the money, you'll still be there."

Connor wasn't quite with him. "As fantasy or reality?"

Nathan smiled with a worldly wisdom Connor had never noticed in him before. "What every good husband becomes—a combination of both."

"Really."

"Trust me."

Connor wondered later as he went upstairs to finish his supplies inventory if that had been his problem with Lisa. Had he not tried hard enough to lend a fantasy element to their lives?

He remembered her complaints about his change of specialties, the blank looks she had given him when he tried to explain how he felt about treating children, her unwillingness to discuss having a family. He finally concluded that while he was most certainly partially to blame, her complaints and criticisms had hardly left room for fantasies to grow.

Then he remembered Shelly sprawled over him in the predawn hours, her hair like silk against his chin, her breath warm and steady against his chest even through his T-shirt, her foot slipping languidly along his bare leg as she obviously dreamed of comfort. After the harsh reality of life with Lisa, last night with Shelly qualified as fantasy—disappointingly unfulfilled fantasy, but fantasy all the same.

He was about to hand Nathan the on-call beeper before grabbing his jacket when the phone rang.

"Hi, Shelly," he heard Nathan say. He turned, wondering if the call was for him. "Yeah, Connor's still here. You want...okay, calm down, Shelly. What...?"

Connor grabbed the phone from him. "What's the matter?" he asked. He could hear Max crying in the background, but the sound of it was almost drowned out by the sound of older children crying. Possibly several of them. Excited adult voices were barking out orders.

"Connor, Luke's trying to get him out, but he's worried about his fingers. They're cold and he's afraid if he can't do it right away and there isn't enough blood flow..."

"Shelly!" He shouted her name to make her stop. "Whose fingers aren't getting any blood flow? Why?"

"Albie Carby! He's stuck in the gum-ball machine!"

He stifled a laugh. It wasn't that the situation was funny; he was sure Albie didn't think so. But compared to the possibilities that had been running through his mind, the gum-ball machine allowed him to smile. "I'm on my way," he said.

He handed Nathan the beeper and grinned. "I know you're officially on call now, but I'm giving you a break. Albie Carby's got his fingers stuck in the gum-ball machine at the Cup. Luke's disassembling the machine, but he's worried about the fingers. Have a good weekend."

"Call me if you need me!"

"Right."

THE CUP WAS ABSOLUTE pandemonium when Shelly saw Connor push his way through the crowd gathered around Luke and Albie and his father. Albie was sobbing, and his younger brothers were crying in apparent sympathy. Ned Carby, who'd already dealt with a very eventful day and had brought the boys to the Cup for dinner while Francie spent the night in the hospital in Pine Run, looked stressed.

Dan knelt beside Luke with a handful of tools, and Shelly stood over them holding Max, who supported the other weeping children with screams of his own.

"Connor!" she exclaimed when she saw him. The name burst out of her, relief filling her at the sight of him. She grabbed him by the arm and pulled him through the layers of onlookers. "He's been stuck for half an hour!"

Luke, lying on his back under the machine, unscrewing the clear ball that held the gum from its metal base, spared him a grin. "Hey, Doc."

"Hey, Sheriff." Connor knelt down beside Albie, who stood trembling, his index and second finger solidly stuck in the machine's dispenser.

"We've tried soap," Luke said, "Vaseline, bacon grease—you name it. Only thing left is taking it apart, but it's a longer job than I expected."

Connor braced a foot on the floor and pulled the boy gently onto his knee. "How you doing, Albie?" he asked, peering into the gum-filled globe, probably trying to see the boy's fingers, but they were covered by the colored balls.

"Is he okay, Doc?" Ned Carby asked. "He's been shaking."

Ned had put his jacket on Albie's shoulders and Connor reached into it to take the pulse of the hand with the stuck fingers.

"It's probably just stage fright," Connor said after listening a moment. "He's got quite an audience. His pulse is fine. Color's good."

Connor grinned at Albie. "You got a black gum ball," he asked, "and reached in to try to get a red one instead?"

Albie stopped crying long enough to nod. "Hate the black ones!"

"Well, when we get the top off, we'll get you a red one. Okay?"

"Okay."

"Can you feel your fingers?"

"Yeah."

"Are they cold?"

"Kinda. And a little sore."

"Tingly?"

"No."

"Shall I get him a cup of cocoa, or something?" Shelly asked.

Connor shook his head. "No. Maybe later. His brothers might like that, though." He indicated the weeping boys with a nod of his head.

"Right. Come on, guys." She shooed Frank and Charlie toward the counter. Irene Caldwell, who'd worked at the bookstore today and come in for dinner before going home, came to take Max from her.

"Let me hold him while you do that," she said.

Shelly handed him over. "Bless you, Irene."

She made strong cocoa, cooled it with an ice cube, then made a mound of whipped cream in each cup and sprinkled it with chocolate jimmies. The boys were diverted from their brother's problem by their excitement over the treat.

While Irene paced with Max, Shelly went back to a chink in the crowd and stood on tiptoe to watch as Luke gave the big globe a twist. It gave.

"Something to put the gum balls in, Shelly!" he shouted.

She ran to get a large bowl and passed it into the crowd. Jack, who'd come over earlier to see what the commotion was and stayed to help, held the bowl under the globe. Luke gave the big plastic ball a turn, then another, and soon gum balls fell noisily into the bowl, sounding a little like firecrackers.

The globe was off, but Albie's fingers remained in the dispenser still attached to the base, just above the pedestal. There was quick applause, then an increase in tension as Connor closed his hands over the two fingers.

"Can you wiggle them?" he asked Albie.

The boy did so but grimaced. "It's tight."

Luke went to work on the screws on the back of the plate holding the dispenser. They were visible now that the globe was off.

"Phillips," he said, handing Dan back the standard screwdriver.

Dan reclaimed it and handed him a Phillips screwdriver, and everyone waited, breath held collectively as Luke worked.

In a moment he had the dispenser free of the pedestal, the boy's fingers still stuck.

"Let's have that soap again, Shelly!" Luke called. "Now that we can work on it from both sides we might get somewhere."

"I brought cold cream!" Sylvia Rutledge, from the hair salon across the street, passed a jar through the crowd.

Luke took it, removed the lid and dipped two fingers. He grimaced and made a sound of disgust. Albie, spirits rising at almost being free, laughed.

Luke slapped a dollop of cream into Connor's hand. He slathered cream all over Albie's fingers from the front and the back of the dispenser that still held him prisoner. Connor helped.

"Towel, Shelly!" Luke called.

Shelly had second-guessed that request and handed him one. He used it to grasp the dispenser.

Connor held the boy to him and took a firm grip on his small palm. "Pull back, Albie," he said. "If it hurts too much, you just say so."

"Okay," he agreed, shutting his eyes tightly in preparation.

Nothing happened on the first try, but on the second effort to pull off the dispenser, it gave with a slick, oily-sounding "Thwack!" and Luke fell onto his backside, holding the piece of metal in his hand.

Albie held up his free fingers with a shout of triumph, and a collective cheer rose from Shelly's customers.

Connor ran his fingertips over the boy's fingers, made him flex them, then stretch, then finally nodded, apparently satisfied that there was no damage beside a little swelling.

"I think he's fine," he told Ned. "But let's take him to the center to x-ray his hand to be sure."

Ned wrapped his arms around his son, then Luke, then Connor. "God, what a day!" he exclaimed. "Okay, boys. Let's go with the doc."

"Wait!" Connor reached for the bowl of gum balls. "After what he's been through, he should have a couple of red ones."

Albie chose several, then his brothers insisted on a few.

With Nathan's help, Albie was soon declared sound

and the Carbys were sent on their way with lollipops to add to their gum ball collection.

When Connor returned to the restaurant, Jack shook his head at Connor over the goings-on. "Aren't you glad you came to Jester?" he asked. "Where else can you get dinner theater over a hamburger?" He and Luke were still reassembling the machine.

"Jack, you're into Kiwanis for nine gum balls," Luke said.

"Me?" Jack protested. "The doc's the one who insisted Albie take them."

"I'm not paying," Connor laughed. "I provided the medical consultation. Luke's the one who took the machine apart and probably won't be able to put it together again."

Luke put a hand to the holster at his side. "You're forgetting who you're talking to, Pilgrim." The words and tone of voice were barely recognizable as a John Wayne impersonation.

Shelly, coming out of the kitchen, rolled her eyes at their playful behavior. "I'll stand for the nine gum balls," she said. "And *if* you two get that back together, there's free pie and coffee for you."

Jack frowned at Luke. "You better know what you're doing." The two turned their complete attention on the project.

Without thinking about what she was doing, Shelly wrapped her arms around Connor's waist and leaned into him. She'd been so glad to see him when he walked in the door. As crises went, it had been a small one, but she'd still felt responsible for its outcome, then felt more sure of a positive one when Connor appeared.

"Thanks for coming so quickly," she said. "We knew we could get him free, but Luke was really worried about his fingers."

Connor squeezed her to him. "It's all right. It could have been a problem for Albie, but, according to the X rays, he's fine. And I was heading this way to pick up the baby, anyway."

Irene waited to pay her bill.

"Dinner's on the house tonight," Shelly said. "Thanks so much for helping with Max."

Irene tucked several small bills into Shelly's apron pocket.

"I said…" Shelly began.

Irene nodded, cutting her off. "I know. Dinner was on the house, and I appreciate that. But good service deserves a tip."

Shelly tried to give her back the money. "And I appreciate *that,* but I've just won—"

"The lottery. Yes, I know. It doesn't change anything." She pinched her cheek. "You take care of that baby." She winked at Connor. "And that man." And she was gone.

Max squealed his delight at nothing in particular and grabbed Shelly by the nose.

Connor laughed and freed her by taking Max. "Can you bring home another piece of coconut cream pie?"

"Sold out," she reported apologetically. "How do you feel about Dutch apple pie?"

"Sounds good. Call me when you leave."

"Okay." She walked him to the door and reached up to kiss him goodbye, this time without thinking twice about it.

Chapter Eight

Connor sat on the floor with Max between his knees, playing with a squeaky toy shaped like a dog. Sean Connery watched them from the safety of a lamp table some distance away, apparently disdainful of the dog-shaped thing. He'd considered the noisy little person doubtful all along, but the squeaky thing had hit him in the head twice. It had achieved enemy status.

After just a few days, Connor noticed that Max sat up a little straighter, wasn't quite as inclined to lean forward. He knew this age was a time when babies changed before your eyes, when they learned something new daily. He'd just never been with one so regularly to see it happen himself.

The time spent with Max underscored his desire for children of his own. And—and though he'd come to terms with this, he still found it difficult to believe—the time spent with Shelly made him believe he could deal with marriage again. He hadn't wanted to, had been sure after the sad turn of events with Lisa, that he wouldn't be able to trust another woman with his dreams for a pediatric clinic of his own. Or, maybe, simply a pediatric practice within the Jester Medical Center.

But he did now. He'd known Shelly less than a week, and though they'd been at odds at first, he'd seen her with Max and understood that what she lacked in knowledge and experience, she more than made up for in caring and enthusiasm. This was more than a crush. More than lust. He was in love.

The telephone rang. He'd placed the cordless phone on the carpet beside him and reached for it without disturbing the baby.

"I'm on my way," Shelly said. "You're sure Dutch apple is okay? There's a pumpkin mousse left."

"Dutch apple's great. Max and I'll watch you from the porch."

"Okay. Five minutes."

"Okay."

He scooped up the baby, went into the kitchen to turn on the coffeepot he'd prepared earlier, then wrapped the baby in a blanket and went out onto the porch.

She was home in five minutes as promised, a small take-out box in her hand. He hung up her coat while she took the baby from him. Max was all smiles at the sight of her, again somehow offended by the sight of her nose and determined to change its location.

She pretended to bite his little fingers and he laughed in a high squeal.

Connor followed her into the kitchen.

Shelly was a bundle of nerves. On one level, she was so comfortable with Connor that it felt as though they'd been married for twenty years.

On another level, she was on the brink of an epiphany and her entire world—her entire being—was aquiver. Everything was against her and Connor having a relationship. As she was always telling him, the restaurant took all her time and she didn't want to be tied down to anyone or anything that might confine her when she finally had the opportunity to *do* things, to *go* places.

But there was no denying what she'd felt when he'd walked into the restaurant tonight. It had been such a simple thing, but her heart had leaped when she'd seen his face, and she'd had a deep-down sense of comfort. He might not be able to affect the whole world, but he had the ability to make a very safe place for her in hers.

Of course, there was always the possibility that he didn't see this thing between them in quite the same way she did. He'd been very candid about his attraction to her, but then he'd actually spent a lot of time with her since then and maybe that had all changed.

He'd been kind, considerate and helpful, but he was a doctor. That was the way he was. And he had a deep affection for Max. Whatever kindness he offered to her might just be an extension of his feelings for the baby.

So she chatted while they had pie and coffee together at the little kitchen table. The baby played with her watch, banged on her arm, then on the table with her spoon so that she and Connor had to shout at each other.

Then Max began to whine and rub his ears. "Getting sleepy," she said, pushing away from the table.

Connor was already up and getting Max's bottle. He ran it under the hot water, then handed it to her.

"I'll clean up in here," he said.

She thanked him and smiled, trying to read what was in his eyes. But they were focused on the plates he was stacking, and she had to guess whether or not he felt any of the tension she felt, if his heart was pounding like hers was.

She took Max into the living room near the fire. He reached for his bottle eagerly and drank with greedy little noises while she rocked slowly back and forth in the wicker chair. His lids swept heavily down, then rose again as he fought sleep. She rocked and hummed softly.

His task finished, Connor came to sit in a corner of the sofa and propped his feet in boot socks on the coffee table. "You're humming the song Dan always plays on the jukebox," he said, casting her a smile.

She nodded. "It's all about a man trying to convince the woman he loves to love him in return."

"Ah, my theme song. How's he doing?"

"Dan?"

"The baby."

"Drifting off."

"Good." He swung his feet to the floor, went to

add more wood to the fire, then took the chenille throw from the back of the sofa and opened it out on the floor. He disappeared into his room and returned with the coverlet off his bed. He dropped it at the foot of the throw.

Shelly watched him with a quickening pulse. "What are you doing?" she whispered.

He went to the sofa beside her for a pillow. His glance chided her pretense at ignorance. "Preparing for what's been in your eyes since I walked into the Cup."

Momentarily off balance because he understood her so completely, she asked with a challenging tilt of her chin, "You're claiming to read my mind?"

He leaned down to kiss her quickly. "No. Your heart," he said, and kissed her again, more slowly. Challenge turned into surrender.

He tossed the pillow at the blanket, then went to the kitchen and returned with the carrier, which he placed on the coffee table. He took Max from her and placed him in it. There was one worrisome moment when Max opened his eyes, but Connor stroked his head and his eyes closed again instantly.

Connor held a hand out to Shelly.

She took it, choosing to forget all her commonsense arguments about the restaurant, her need to be free. Sure and steady Shelly was taking a walk on the wild side. The life she'd been comfortable in for so long— the life she'd *understood*—now seemed to bear no resemblance to the life in which she found herself. And, at least for this moment, she was as different from the old Shelly as though she were someone else.

She let Connor lead her to the blanket then looped her arms around his neck as he placed his hands at her waist. They looked into each other's eyes. His were clear and deep, like walking into a meadow that extended forever.

He smiled. "You look worried," he observed.

"I'm not," she denied. "It's just...*I'm* just... different than I usually am. I feel..." She groped for the right word.

"What?" he prodded, putting a hand to her hair.

If she'd had trouble clarifying what she felt before, his touch made it even more difficult. She closed her eyes and leaned into his hand, struggling to think.

"Um...I feel...unlike myself," she said finally.

He dropped his hand to her shoulder. She opened her eyes to find that *he* looked worried. "But it's the Shelly I know that I want to make love with."

She shrugged artlessly. "Well, the Shelly you know hasn't felt like herself since the day you walked into my life. Or, I guess, I walked into yours."

"Really." He frowned. "What changed?"

"Everything," she admitted. "My life was safe, but you aren't."

He dropped both hands from her and folded his arms, his expression more troubled. "I feel like a threat to you?"

"Not to me." She undid his arms, hating that he no longer touched her. Then she stepped into them and wrapped hers around his waist. "To my peace of mind. To my concept of how things are. To what I want."

His arms closed around her again, but tentatively. "What do you want?" he asked.

She tightened her hold on him and said with sincere emphasis, "I want you, Connor."

HE'D DESPAIRED of ever hearing her admit it. The words were like silk running over his skin. He praised her with kisses, drew her sweater up and off, and rained them all over her throat, her shoulders, her clavicle.

He found one small hook on the scrap of white lace that covered her breasts and unfastened it. He tossed it aside with the sweater and cupped his hands over the small but firm globes. Their tips pearled against his palm and he stroked them with his thumbs.

She expelled a breath and a small sound that reminded him of Sean Connery in high purr.

She drew away to unbutton his shirt, then pulled it and his T-shirt off with flattering determination. They stood wrapped in each other's arms and reveled a moment in the delicious sensation of being flesh to flesh.

Then he drew her down with him to the blanket, relieved her of her corduroy slacks and white lace panties, and put his lips to her flat stomach. He thought absently that she was smaller than the impression she made.

He felt her hands in his hair, her bare knee against

his side. She urged him onto his back, worked at his belt and his zipper, and had him free of jeans and shorts with the same efficiency he'd employed on her.

Her eyes ran over him, a blush coloring her cheeks as she raised her gaze to look into his. He guessed the blush had more to do with surprise at her own behavior than embarrassment.

Her hair fell over her face as she braced herself astride him and he tucked it behind her left ear. "You usually do this with your eyes closed?" he teased gently.

She met his eyes frankly. "I usually don't do this, period," she said with a shrug that was hard to accomplish with her arms braced against the floor. "I mean, I *have* done it, but I'm friends with most of the single men in town, so that doesn't work. And strangers aren't safe, so the opportunities aren't really… plentiful." Her finger traced the line of his earlobe. "I suppose you do it all the time."

"Not as often as you'd think." He put a hand to the back of her thigh, fascinated by the cool silk of it. "I work a lot, I'm aware of being safe and selective, too, and contrary to what women tell each other, it isn't the only thing guys think about. Unless they meet a woman who really catches their attention and then, yes, thoughts of lovemaking choke out everything else."

She seemed amused by that admission. "And what have you been thinking about?" she asked.

"Oh, let's see." He ran both hands up her rib cage,

then lifted her slightly to break her contact with the floor and lowered her to his chest so that they were flesh to flesh again, her breasts squashed against his chest, their legs entangled. "I've imagined making love to you on my cot upstairs in the medical center, in the back row of the movie theater, in my car, and right here, just like this."

She raised her head to smile at him. "In the back of the movie theater?"

He nodded. "I went there the first two nights I was here."

"But the movie changes only once a week."

"I know. I saw *Gosford Park* twice. Incidentally, why is there duct tape on the screen?"

She grinned. "Dev threw a bottle rocket through it when he was a kid. I guess there's just never been enough money to have it repaired or get another screen. Movie theaters are hurting all over the country, and they stay alive by charging a fortune for candy and popcorn. But not ours. So we live with the duct tape."

"Sure."

"You didn't like the movie enough to see it a third time?"

"I liked it a lot. But I met you on the third day and came home with you, remember? I just went to bed and dreamed of making love to you amid all those British accents."

"But you didn't like me."

"I had the hots for you, anyway."

She slapped his chest and he held her close, laughing. Then he rolled them so that she lay beside him, her back to the fireplace.

"I went from thinking you were the most incompetent woman with a baby I'd ever seen, to falling in love with you. I mean falling—like off a cliff or a bridge."

"I love you, too," she said, as though that reality confounded her. "I don't know what to do about it, but I do."

"Do you have to do something about it?"

"Isn't love supposed to encourage you to make decisions about your life?"

"I think it's just supposed to heighten the life you're already living."

"Well, it is doing that." She smiled in a way he found sweetly ingenuous.

"I'm glad to hear that." He put a hand to her stomach and drew her to him with the arm that rested under her shoulders. "This is what I feel encouraged to do. Be quiet, please, and give me your full attention."

She did. It would have been hard to do otherwise when his fingertips found every erotic zone she possessed and brought it artfully to full awareness. It occurred to her to wonder if it was unusual that one woman had so many—several of which she hadn't even known about—but the thought went unexplored when he found yet another and she had to concentrate on drawing every breath so that she didn't faint with each progressively erotic discovery.

Fulfillment had never been an easy accomplishment for her. And given the infrequency of her opportunities lately, even the last attempt had been some time ago.

It astonished her that she didn't have to work for this one. She didn't have to wait and wonder and accept disappointment. It just rode over her with the same style he'd applied in the exploration of her body. It rocked her. It found every sensitive little nook and cranny in her body and stirred the responses there until they met at the heart of her in one cosmic, rolling implosion.

She felt herself shudder, heard herself cry out. Connor's hand closed gently over her mouth. Still in the throes of it, she wondered if he was worried about waking the baby—or possibly the neighborhood.

She hadn't known she was a screamer. Hadn't known she had eleventy-seven places on her body that went wild when touched. Hadn't known she could feel as though she lay in a bath of stars.

"Hey," Connor said, patting her hip, his voice soft but rich with amusement. "Are you still with me?"

She tried to raise her head, but it fell with a thunk against his shoulder. "I hope so," she breathed. "I hate to think that's the last time I'll ever feel like that."

"It isn't. Want to feel like that again?"

"Yes."

"Now?"

"Yes."

He put his hand to one of those dynamite points, but she came to sufficiently to catch it and stop him.

"Wait," she said, trying to collect herself. "You're coming with me this time."

"Okay," he said, "but you've got some catching up to do." His hand went back to that wild pulse point and she felt it all coming on again, even quicker than before.

She closed her hand over him and nudged him onto his back.

"Okay," he said in a strained voice. "Maybe not so much catching up."

She kissed him everywhere he'd touched her and a few places unique to him alone. She blew air in a little breath down the middle of his body, then kissed her way up again until she reached his mouth.

He tried to lay her down but she resisted him, tracing kisses across his shoulders and following with her fingernail, as though she strummed an instrument.

"Shelly…" he pleaded.

"Yes, Connor?" She was planting kisses on his chest, nipping at his ribs.

He took her firmly by the waist, lay her down beside him, and while she smiled into his eyes with deep satisfaction and anticipation, he entered her with one confident move and erased every other thought from her mind but the perfection of their union.

The world rocked—literally and figuratively. What she'd experienced before seemed magnified several times by the fact that he'd experienced it with her. His gasps and tremors contributed to hers, his pounding heartbeat was one with hers, their hold on each other made it impossible to tell whose flesh tingled.

It was a moment before she recovered. No, not recovered. It was a moment before she was herself again. She doubted that she'd ever recover from making love with Connor. She hadn't intended to erase the old life, but she felt as though that was what had happened. Oh, she had all her precious memories, maintained all the love her parents had given her, and the friendships she'd made in Jester, but *she* was different.

And while she hadn't known a moment's fear when turning this corner into a relationship with Connor, she experienced a moment's trepidation now. Change! This was the change she'd been so worried about when Jester won the lottery. But it wasn't the lives of everyone else that had changed.

It was hers.

She sank into an exhausted heap against Connor and accepted that.

CONNOR WAS A LITTLE SURPRISED by the emotional impact of making love with Shelly. He'd lusted after her body for days, knew his feelings for her were growing hourly, accepted that the safe bachelorhood he'd promised himself for the rest of his life was down the tubes. He'd known that loving her would present a challenge that could alter his life. What if she truly didn't want children? Could he choose between having her and having children?

Loving her had quieted him, and he'd managed to forget the cursed O'Rourke determination that had driven one ancestor to kidnap an English bride when her father refused to give him her hand in marriage, and encouraged another to escape the potato famine and take a ship to New York with nothing but hope in his pocket. That same determination had made Connor, himself, turn his entire life around when he discovered he loved working with children.

His stubbornness lived, and it convinced him that he could have Shelly *and* he could have children if he was simply resourceful enough to figure out how.

The answer, he thought with sudden inspiration as he reached for his coverlet and pulled it over both of them, rested in little Max.

Chapter Nine

"We'll adopt him," he said to Shelly matter-of-factly as he followed her to the monument on the Town Hall lawn. She had a tour guide attitude this Sunday morning, and a digital camera in hand. He spoke lightly so that she wouldn't panic. "His mother's apparently not coming back, and now that we've cared for him this long, and have the backing of the sheriff and Jester's family practitioner, I don't see how they can turn us down."

She stopped in front of the statue and turned to face him, shielding her eyes from the bright sun. It was a brilliant day with clear blue skies and not a cloud in sight. The temperature, though, was still in the single digits so the snow remained firm.

"You're serious?" she asked.

He was pleased by the fact that she seemed only mildly surprised. She was vastly different this morning from the woman he'd met five days ago.

Five days! he thought in amazement. Had it been

only five days? Destiny, he guessed, is what made it feel as though it had been forever.

She seemed less volatile, steadier, yet there was a new sort of concern about her that worried him. He knew she'd found last night as life altering as he had, but she'd emerged from it with a curious quiet that made him just a little nervous.

He might be alarming himself over nothing. She'd been staring at him when he awoke this morning, made love with him eagerly again, made him breakfast with a song on her lips, and suggested this outing together with obvious anticipation and good cheer.

As a doctor, though, he had good instincts. He'd learned to read information that wasn't spoken aloud: he read eyes; he read between the lines. He should simply ask her about it, but he guessed she'd pushed it aside this morning, and he didn't want to do anything to startle her into thinking that taking up with him had been a bad idea.

So he was going to wait it out.

"I'm very serious," he replied. He had Max in a backpack—another loan from the Perkinses—and the baby pointed a mittened finger at the statue and squealed.

She grinned and shot a picture of him and the pointing baby. "You haven't asked me to marry you."

"I don't have to," he said, moving forward to read the plaque. "When I got up with him last night so you could stay snuggled under the covers, you proposed to *me*. 'Dedicated to the memory of Catherine

Peterson, horsewoman and humanitarian, and Jester, the buckskin range horse who made us famous.' Famous,'' Connor repeated consideringly. ''That's overstated just a little, don't you think?'' He looked up to see Catherine in a shirt and britches, a wide-brimmed hat dangling on her back from a cord around her throat. Despite the bronze that had gone green with time and the need for a good cleaning, her features were strong and beautiful. She sat determinedly astride the bucking horse, which looked as wild and exquisite as the woman.

Shelly laughed and rolled her eyes. ''I said you were so handy to have around I was going to keep you. And, no, I don't think it's overstated. At least, during the Spanish-American War, it wasn't. Jester sired a whole line of surefooted cow ponies that served the United States Army.''

''Keep me, marry me. Same difference. I read in Mrs. Hollis's book that Catherine tamed Jester when none of the local men could.''

''True. She had a gift—with horses and with people.''

''Are any of Jester's descendants still around?''

''The Petersons have a couple. I work all the time,'' she reminded him.

He nodded. ''And yet we managed to watch a baby and have a life. I think it'll work.''

''You do?''

''I do. See? We're already rehearsing wedding vows.''

She kissed him lightly on the lips. "You're so cute. Now, get out of the way so I can take the picture."

Connor stepped out of the way, catching Max's little hand as he pointed and squealed again. "Horse," Connor said, pointing. "Horse."

Max pointed and squealed something indecipherable.

The picture taken, Shelly indicated the little white church next door with its tall spire and country church simplicity. The roof was in obvious disrepair, with quite a few shingles missing.

"Pastor Brooks says he's afraid to hammer in new shingles," Shelly explained, "afraid it'll make the whole roof collapse." She stepped back into the middle of the street and took a picture.

"Nice little place to get married," Connor said with a casual smile. "Would look wonderful in our wedding album."

She gave him a scolding look. "You're obsessing."

He smiled impenitently. "Yes. Where to next?"

She pointed to the streetlight on the corner right behind him. "We used to have flower baskets there once upon a time. I think it'd be neat if we did that again."

"What do you do in winter?"

"Seasonal ornaments. Last year, Amanda made a witch out of an old mannequin's body, put high heels on it and a broom under it and made it look as though she'd smashed into the pole. Required no head, just a witch's hat askew. Made everyone laugh. We could do those all up and down the street. And, of course, Christmas ornaments, hearts for Valentine's Day, bunnies for Easter, then it's warm enough to put up the baskets.''

"Sounds good."

"I'm just a fountain of great ideas," she boasted teasingly and caught his hand to lead him across Megabucks Boulevard to Main Street. "Come on. We're heading for the park."

They photographed dead flower beds, bleachers that were much the worse for wear, and a wooden pavilion near a pond that looked as though it had seen better days.

She dragged him behind the bleachers and across the street to Jester Public School. She pointed to the empty playground. "The playground equipment was so old that it was no longer up to code. The kids are spending all their recess time at the park. Which isn't bad for the bigger kids, but the smaller ones need monkey bars, sandboxes, that kind of stuff."

"Makes sense to me."

"Okay. Come on. I'll show you the old Victorian on the next block."

"Good grief," he said. "You're going to fix that, too?"

"No," she replied. "I just think it's neat. I think the mayor wants to buy it, but the title isn't clear or something. I don't know what the problem is. It's been empty for a long time."

Connor studied the crumbling old house while

Shelly took several pictures. He had to agree with her. It was the kind of house you wanted to know more about, the kind of place that suggested a history that had to be fascinating.

She walked him back to the corner and pointed down the block to a vacant building. "Auto repair shop," she said. "When I was little, I used to think I'd like to work there because you probably didn't have to wash dishes. But as I grew older I realized there probably were a lot of other ugly jobs I wouldn't want to do."

He nodded. "The grass is always greener. It's just human nature."

She hooked her arm in his as they walked up Lottery Lane to Orchard Street. "Okay, I've got my pictures. What do you want to do now?"

"Want to go to the movies at four?"

"Haven't you already seen it twice?"

"It changed on Friday."

"What about Max?"

"We'll sedate him and take him with us."

"Connor!" She looked horrified.

He laughed and teased her for believing he'd do that. "We'll bring a bottle, his pacifier, all that stuff and if he gets too fussy, we'll leave. He's been awake for hours, got lots of fresh air, he should sleep for a couple of hours. This could work."

"What's playing?" she asked, catching her hat as Max pulled it off her head. "You're not taking me to some war or horror thing, are you?"

"No, it was a Julia Roberts movie, I believe."

She brightened. "Really? And that's okay with you?"

"Yeah. Why *wouldn't* I want to see Julia Roberts?"

She punched his arm playfully. "Because you claim to be in love with me."

"But looking is different from…"

She tightened her grip on his arm. "It's not," she corrected. "So, if we ever were to get married, don't go thinking you can look at all the pretty girls and I won't get upset."

All right! She was thinking about it.

"Jealousy's very sexy in a woman."

"You won't think so when I hit you with a frying pan."

The movie appeared to be a serious story about love between a dedicated career woman and a witty, charming man who had a terminal illness. Until the heroine discovered that the hero had lied about being ill. It was a tool he used regularly with women to avoid commitment. His pretended illness solicited the care and cosseting of his female companions, while saving him from having to promise himself to a relationship.

Until the heroine discovered his deceit and the story became a romp as she did all in her power to encourage him to marry her, insisting that she loved him so much that when he was close to death, they would leap off the Golden Gate Bridge hand in hand.

He finally confessed his trickery, she admitted to

her ruse, and they went their separate ways, angry with each other's machinations.

He looked at the phone as though wanting to call her, and she was preoccupied at a board meeting, thinking of him. Their relationship was about to resolve itself when Max woke up with a vengeance. He didn't want his bottle or the pacifier or to be held.

"I'll take him outside and wait for you," Connor whispered as everyone in the theater looked their way.

"No, I'll come with you," she insisted, gathering up their things.

"No, stay."

"No. We're in this together."

"So, what do you think happened?" Connor asked as they walked home, Max now happy to be outdoors and exclaiming at the stars.

"He apologized abjectly," she speculated, "and promised to give her whatever she wanted if she married him."

"I think he made her promise to work less and enjoy life more," he countered, "and if she agreed, he asked her to marry him."

She stopped indignantly in her tracks. "He lied about dying! That's awful!"

"That's true." He moved on and she followed. "But he wanted to get to know her, and it was the only way he could get her to slow down enough to accomplish that, to let her get to know him. She was working day and night, completely oblivious to her life. It was more like *she* was dying."

She thought that over. "I guess we're going to have to agree to be split along gender lines on this one."

"Love scene was good, though," he said, catching Max's hand as he banged it against his face.

She made a scornful sound. "You can't make love in a bathtub."

He raised an eyebrow. "You most certainly can."

Now she raised an eyebrow. "You've done it?"

"Yes." He said it firmly.

"And you didn't freeze or drown?"

"Obviously not. I'm still here."

"Mmm." She wandered on beside him, her hands in her pockets. "I always thought it was something they just did in the movies so great bodies could be shown almost naked. I mean, I can understand a hot tub, but with a bathtub, you've got faucets and drain plugs. I don't see…"

He hooked his free arm around her shoulders and pulled her closer. "Well, you will," he said, "once you've had a little field experience."

"WELL, I'LL BE DARNED," Shelly said breathlessly just before midnight when she lay atop Connor's body in the old ball and claw bathtub off her bedroom. Max slept in the carrier in her bedroom beyond the open bathroom door.

They'd just made love in a confined but deliciously powerful way, the experience heightened by the lap of French-lavender-scented water against their bodies and the flickering light of a single candle on a small shelf.

Connor sat up and turned her so that she sat between his knees. "Tuck your feet in," he advised, then reached out with his long foot to turn on the hot water.

She felt it work its way through their now-tepid suds, warming the water around them. She leaned back against him with a sigh of contentment. He scooped up a dollop of suds with his index finger and dropped it on her nose.

"Now I'm going to smell like a girl," he complained on a teasing note. She noticed that, despite the complaint, he didn't seem inclined to move out of the scented water.

"Dean'll spritz some manly stuff on you if you stop at the barbershop."

"I go to work two hours before he opens."

"Whine, whine," she said, flicking water behind her and into his face. "If you didn't want to do this, you should have just said so."

"Hey!" He pinched her hip. "You should have warned me that you were putting stuff in the water."

She leaned sideways to turn and look at him. He was sexily disheveled, the tips of his hair wet, the effects of their lovemaking still in his eyes. "You were in here with me when I did it!" she reminded him. "Remember? You had my shirt in your hand and I asked you to give me a minute so I could—"

"I was distracted, okay?" he interrupted with a

grin. "And I was just trying to contribute to your collective life experience."

"You were trying to seduce me."

"Didn't I just say that?"

She slapped the water to splash him and, as he moved to retaliate, water sloshed out of the tub and extinguished the candle.

They lay back, laughing, then made love again in the dark.

"LOUISE IS COMING on Wednesday," Nathan told Shelly and Connor on Monday afternoon. Shelly had closed the coffee shop and walked with Max to the medical center to pick up Connor. Nathan was on call tonight. "I talked to Luke this morning and he still has nothing on Max's mother. I don't think we'll be able to stall CFS any longer."

Shelly felt her stomach tighten and her throat close.

She hated the thought of giving up the baby. She looked down at his wide-eyed, pink-cheeked little face staring into hers and felt tears bite her eyes.

"I'm going to ask her if I can keep him," she said, avoiding Connor's eyes. "Do you think that could happen?"

Nathan looked uncertain. "They have a long list of couples waiting to adopt. Couples who've been interviewed and checked out. I don't know, Shelly. And I'm not sure they can make him available for adoption until they know what's happened to his mother."

"What about my keeping him as a foster parent?"

"I don't know. I'm sure Louise can give you all the details, though."

"Okay." She turned to Connor, heavyhearted. After the wonderful weekend they'd shared, she felt real concern today over what to do about their relationship. It had been on her mind all day. "You ready to go?"

He'd changed out of his lab coat, and wore a dark blue parka over jeans and a sweatshirt. She expected him to be angry because she was discussing the possibility of adopting Max without having talked it over with him, without accepting or rejecting his suggestion that they get married.

Instead, he looked curiously detached, as though not caring one way or the other. After what they'd shared over the weekend, she was sure it had to be an act. At least, she hoped it was.

CONNOR WANTED TO RANT. He had an overwhelming urge to shout and throw things. He wanted to grab Shelly and shake her until the fog she lived under disappeared.

But he was beginning to think that wasn't going to happen. If their weekend of lovemaking hadn't convinced her that they were made for each other, he didn't know what could. The trouble was, it had convinced *him*. He forced himself to stay calm until he could figure out what to do about it.

He took the carrier with Max in it from Shelly as they walked home. She tucked her hand in his free arm.

"If I accepted your proposal now," she said, "you'd think it was because I wanted Max. I've been thinking about this all day. I don't believe we should decide anything about us until we know what's going to happen with him."

His calm slipped, but he struggled to hold on to it. "I think it would help you to get Max if we were married," he said. "But what I feel for you has nothing to do with him."

"But you'd question *my* feelings."

"No, I wouldn't," he insisted as they stopped at the corner of Orchard, waiting for a pickup truck to pass. "*You're* questioning your feelings. And you're trying to blame it on me."

The truck passed, but they remained on the corner as their argument continued.

"I'm not blaming anything on you!" she replied a little hotly. "I just don't think we can leap into anything on five days' acquaintance with a baby involved. You want to make it happen because you want the family Lisa wouldn't give you."

"And you *don't* want it," he snapped back, "because if your parents didn't do it first, or it isn't okayed by the people of Jester, you don't know what to do about anything!"

She stared at him in hurt surprise as his words circled them on the early evening air. A block behind them, light traffic passed on Main Street, people greeted each other, a horn honked and somewhere a dog barked. But on the corner of Lottery Lane and Orchard Street, war had broken out.

Connor might have taken the words back given the chance, but he knew they'd have to be said sometime if he was ever going to have a life with Shelly. He expelled a sigh, ran a hand over his face and caught her arm. "Come on," he said. "We'll finish this at home."

In the living room, he took Max out of the carrier and put him on a throw on the floor while Shelly went to the refrigerator for a bottle. She was back with it in a few minutes.

He was still building a fire when she came to stand over him.

"Were you implying that I'm unable to make up my own mind?" she demanded.

"Yeah," he replied, touching a match to the kindling and twisted paper and watching to see if it would take.

He half expected the tennis shoe he could see out of the corner of his right eye to boot him right into the fireplace. But she paced around to his other side instead.

"And what in the hell makes you think you know that much about me after less than a week? You're just judgmental and opinionated! And egotistical! My first impression of you was right on!"

The flame licked at the firewood and finally caught. He pushed himself to his feet, repositioned the fireplace screen, then turned to her, braced to do battle.

She stood just a few feet from him, apparently girded to do the same. If the strength in her body could match the fire in her eyes, he suspected he'd be in danger of serious injury.

"Think about it," he said, making himself keep his voice down. He glanced at the playpen and saw that Max was sitting up straight, bottle in hand, watching them. He wished circumstances were different so they could focus on that little victory together. But they weren't. "Think about your arguments for not getting involved. You work all the time, and you want to be free to take advantage of the opportunities afforded by your winnings."

"And?" she asked imperiously.

"And they're diametrically opposed arguments," he said. "You claim that you work all the time, so I can't lay claim to your regular time, and you claim that you want to be free to take off on a moment's notice, so I can't lay claim to your free time. You don't want to give me anything. You want to stay all alone making stew and waiting tables because that's what your parents always did and that's what makes you comfortable."

"I want Max!"

"Sure you do, because he's a way to have a child without actually having to let anyone else into your life—except the baby. It's perfect."

"You're just angry," she fired back, "because it's possible I'd be able to get him without involving you!" Her eyes filled with tears, probably more anger than grief, as she went on. "You wedged your way into my life thinking I wouldn't be able to get him without you and you'd finally have your family. You thought poor, incompetent Shelly wouldn't be able to manage without you, but I can. I can!"

It amazed him how quickly their argument had deteriorated. He could only imagine she felt as wounded as he did and there was nothing to be gained by prolonging it.

And by all indications, there was nothing to be gained by his staying.

He grabbed the jacket he'd tossed over the back of the sofa. "You're absolutely right," he said quietly. "You've learned to cope with Max very well. You don't need me anymore." He jammed his hands into his pocket and connected in the right one with the pacifier that often ended up there. He took it out and handed it to her.

She frowned darkly at him, then came forward and snatched it from him.

"If he cries during the night, you now know all the tricks I know. If he does get sick or hurt, you know how to reach me." He went to the blanket and squatted down to plant a kiss on the baby's head. A pudgy little fist dropped the bottle and reached for him. He squeezed the tiny fingers, then headed for the door.

"Connor!" she called as he pulled it open.

He turned coolly, waiting, secretly hoping she would fling herself at him and tell him she hadn't meant any of it.

She hesitated, opened her mouth, closed it, took a step forward then stopped. "Thank you for your help," she said finally, stiffly.

"Sure," he replied in the same tone, and left.

Later, holding the baby on her hip, Shelly stirred soup and tried to figure out what had happened. Not that it required much investigation. They'd yelled and screamed at each other, hurled accusations, then told each other they weren't needed, that's what happened.

Well. Not exactly. She'd told him she didn't need him. He'd told her she was unable to make any serious decisions in her life.

"Well, that's just not true!" she told Max as she ladled soup into a mug. He reached for the ladle and she held it out of his reach, getting soup all over the counter. She didn't let herself think about how much easier it was to get dinner when Connor was entertaining Max.

She put him in the carrier on the table and endured his screaming while she wiped up the mess, turned off the burner and tried to eat her soup. She put a few Cheerios in Max's hand, hoping they'd entertain him, but he simply threw them.

She gave up after she'd eaten half the soup, then played with Max on the floor near the fire, telling herself it was just as well. Connor had created turmoil in her life from the moment she'd met him anyway, and the Duprees always worked hard but strove for a quiet life.

Quiet lives, a little voice told her, required little decision making.

She ignored the voice and rolled the large ball at Max, who gave it a sharp, uncoordinated smack that struck the pot of flowers she'd bought herself the day she deposited her lottery winnings. The vase broke and spewed flowers and water all over.

Curiously, it didn't seem to matter.

Max, startled by the noise, began to cry. She sat with him in the rocker until he went to sleep. She placed him on the sofa while she cleaned up the mess, then put him down in the crib upstairs and prepared for bed.

Then she remembered that she hadn't turned off the lights and locked up. She'd grown accustomed to Connor doing that.

She fought the surge of tears in her throat and her eyes, cleared her throat, swallowed, then went downstairs to take care of the details she'd always done herself before anyway.

When she climbed into bed, she lay on her back the way she used to sleep, rather than on her side, curled into Connor. A minute later she couldn't remember why she'd ever thought that comfortable, and turned onto her side. Her nose landed on the edge of the pillow Connor had used last night and caught a whiff of French lavender.

She burst into tears, pulled the pillow to her and sobbed into it.

Chapter Ten

"I thought I heard something up here," Nathan said, standing in the doorway of the storage room in a thick sweater and jeans. "What are you doing? I thought you left with Shelly and the baby?"

Nathan, who'd gone home for dinner when Connor returned to the medical center, was obviously back to work on the books, judging by the folder under his arm. Connor reclined on his cot with an old *Sports Illustrated.*

"We had a parting of the ways," Connor replied. "Why don't you go home to Vickie. I'll be here tonight anyway, so I'll take call."

Nathan came to sit on a stack of boxes facing him. "What do you mean, a parting of the ways? Over her wanting the baby?"

"No." Connor closed the magazine, swung his legs over the side of the cot and sat up. "Over her not wanting me."

"Oh," Nathan said grimly. "Are you sure, though?

Vickie said when she delivered the playpen, she thought Shelly looked like she had a crush on you.''

Crush. Connor smiled, remembering the word he'd once used. It was pretty small compared to what he felt now.

"If she did," he said, "she's gotten over it."

"You know…" Nathan stared at the floor as though thinking how to frame what he had to say. He used to do that in medical school, Connor remembered. Take a while to put his thoughts together, then come out with a beautifully organized argument for his position, whatever it was. "Shelly's parents were the salt of the earth, but that girl had no childhood. She was always working. She never had a boyfriend because she worked weekends, and when she went away to school, she had to come back because her mother got sick. She probably wouldn't know what to do with fun if it ran over her."

Connor nodded. "Yeah. She told me all that. She thinks I care about her only because she has Max and it's my chance to get the family Lisa wouldn't give me."

"Is it?"

"No." That was honest. "Though I rushed her, I guess, because I know I love her. And I'd like to have her for myself. So I guess that is selfish after all."

"Of course it's not selfish. Love wants to claim! That's the way it works. I think you probably represent everything she's ever dreamed of during the long hours she's spent in that kitchen at the coffee shop, and she's probably afraid to trust that you're real. And now she's got all this money she isn't sure what to do with, and she isn't sure she deserves that when her parents struggled their whole lives. I think she's just a sweet, smart girl in an unfamiliar situation and she's panicking.''

Frankly, Connor was weary of trying to figure out what was happening with Shelly. "You think she'll be able to get Max?''

"I really don't know. I'll vouch for her, of course, but while Louise gave us some slack this week, she's usually a stickler for doing things by the book.''

Connor nodded. He hated to think Shelly and Max would be separated. For a woman who'd been completely at a loss when she'd walked into his office with the baby, she now handled him very well and was learning every day.

"Go home to Vickie,'' Connor said again, "so I can get some sleep if I do get called out tonight.''

"Connor…''

"Go. I'm going to be up anyway. I may as well be productive.''

"If you're sure.''

"I'm sure.''

Nathan left and Connor spent the next few hours restocking the two examining rooms. Then he spotted the current *Pine Run Plain Talker* on Nathan's desk and took it upstairs with him to get serious about finding a house. Something with a fireplace, he thought, remembering playing with Max on the carpet in front of Shelly's. Something with a garage or a shed big enough to house a shop—like Shelly's father's old shop. Something old with a ball and claw tub like...

He fought the image that tried to form in his mind as he remembered making love to her in the bathtub. But it was so woven into his senses, into his memory, that it came without his consent. He saw himself stretched out in the water, his knees bent because he was longer than the tub. Shelly astride him, water dripping from the tips of her hair, clinging to the curve of her shoulders and breasts as she took him inside her, her hazel eyes caressing his face with love and wonder.

He balled the newspaper into his hands and threw it across the crowded storage room. He went back downstairs, made a pot of coffee and searched the small refrigerator Nathan kept there for something to eat. He found a cup of blueberry yogurt and half a bagel.

It was going to be a very long night.

SHELLY DROVE the one block to work Tuesday morning because she hadn't slept a wink and was already exhausted.

Dan took one look at her and suggested she call in Betsy Wagner, a single woman in her middle twenties, who occasionally waited tables when Shelly had to be away.

"Thanks, but I'm fine," she said, placing Max in the playpen.

"You guys have a fight?" he asked gently.

"Yes," she replied testily, "and that's all I'm going to say about it." She glanced at the clock. "Dean and his friends will be here any minute, Dan. We don't have time to chat."

He accepted her rebuff with a nod and turned back to the grill he was warming.

She was halfway to the counter when conscience drove her back. "I'm sorry," she said, putting a hand to his shoulder. "I didn't mean to take it out on you. I just can't talk about it or I won't be able to get through the day."

"It's okay," he said. "I understand."

She put the first pot of coffee on the warming plate and, knowing it'd be gone in a heartbeat when Dean and his friends arrived, she made a second pot.

Dean, Finn and Henry arrived and placed their orders, and she filled the pastry tray while waiting for Dan to tell her it was up.

She stacked two plates on her arm and one in her free hand as she'd done a million times before and started toward the back booth. She was halfway there when she went down.

She had no idea what happened. She didn't feel herself trip or slip, she simply went down, eggs, bacon, hot butter, French toast sliding off the plates and onto her body and face.

"Oh, my God!"

"Shelly!"

"Dan!"

Shelly was less embarrassed than stunned when Dean and his friends helped her up. Dan came running from the kitchen, pulled a nearby chair out and sat her down.

"I *told* you you shouldn't be here," he said. "Are you all right? You need to see the doc?"

"No!" she said a little more sharply than necessary. Then she repeated it again more calmly. "No. I just…I don't know. Slipped or something." She looked apologetically at her favorite long-time customers. "I'm sorry, guys. Dan'll get your order right up again while I clean—"

Dan caught her arm and dragged her toward the kitchen. "I'm calling Betsy. Get cleaned up, you're going home."

Before she could object, he dialed the phone.

As she tried to think of an argument, Dean went to the back of the kitchen, grabbed the mop and a spray cleaner and carried them both back into the restaurant. Finn and Henry passed him on their way to the kitchen with broken plates and all the food she'd dropped collected on the empty pastry tray she'd left on the counter.

So she wasn't needed. Apparently not by anyone.

"Dean, will you drive her home?" Dan asked as he hung up the phone. "Betsy's on her way in."

"But I drove in this morning," she shouted as she hurried toward the bathroom to change into an old pair of sweats she kept there for cleanup.

"I'll drive you home in your car," Dean shouted,

"and walk back. But hurry up. I want to actually *eat* my breakfast this time."

"Ha! Ha!" she retorted, dropping her clothes and apron into a plastic bag she handed to Dean. Then she scooped up the baby, and they trooped out to her car.

Dean had her home in a minute, carried the baby into the kitchen for her and placed the carrier on the table. "You're sure you don't need to see the doc?" he asked.

"I'm sure," she replied, putting Max in the playpen in the middle of the kitchen floor.

"Okay." He gave her a quick hug. "You always work too hard. Relax, okay? Now you can afford to hire help, you know."

She walked him to the door. "Thanks, Dean. Sorry about your breakfast."

"It's okay. I just wish I'd had my camera. It's too bad Harvey Brinkman missed that move."

She swatted his shoulder as he headed down the steps.

Shelly closed the door behind him and headed back to the kitchen, where Max sat up straight, completely occupied with a squeak toy. He shook it, threw it, then picked up the pacifier on the mat beside him. He put it in his mouth and looked up at her, pleased with his own accomplishment. He grinned around the plastic disk.

Her heart swelled with love. In the brief six days she'd cared for him, he seemed to have developed so much. She put dry Cheerios in a bowl she put down beside him, and while he concentrated on getting one from the bowl to his mouth, wondering what to do with it since there was already a pacifier there, she looked into the refrigerator, trying to find something to fix for herself.

She had decided on stew, despite the early hour, when there was a knock at the front door.

She went to it, hoping it was Connor prepared to apologize for last night's argument.

It wasn't.

A tall young man, probably in his late twenties, stood there in jeans and a short denim jacket. His hair was a little too long and looked as though it hadn't been washed in a while. He had thickly lashed blue eyes that lingered on her a moment, then darted past her into the room. He smiled.

"Miss Dupree?" he asked.

She couldn't account for her sudden sense of unease, but it was there. She kept her hand firmly on the half-open door.

"Yes?"

"I'm Max, Senior," he said. "My little wife abandoned our baby, but I don't hold with ignoring your kin. I've come to take him home."

Her heart punched against her ribs. She looked into the man's face, searching for family resemblance. Of course, that was difficult to find in a baby so young, even if it existed.

"Really," she said, trying to buy time. "Well, I'm sorry, but Max isn't here. The sheriff has him."

A cloud darkened the man's expression, lending it a suddenly frightening quality. Then another man who'd apparently been hiding against the side of the house, stepped out beside him.

There she did detect a family resemblance to the Max, Senior, in the dirty hair and the dark expression. His brother?

"Now, the lady workin' at the coffee shop told us you'd brought the baby home."

Her composure was holding by a thread. "Well, she was mistaken. Now, if you'll excuse me…"

As she began to close the door, a loud baby squeal came from the kitchen.

The first man kicked the door out of her hand and reached for her. She took off at a run for the kitchen, but he caught her by the back of her shirt.

"Now, we don't want any trouble," he said, his voice polite though his grip was vicious. "We just want the baby."

"You're not his father!" she said, struggling against his hold.

"Now, you don't know that," he said. "And you told a reporter that you opened a bank account for the baby for $50,000 for his education. You and me are goin' to the bank and put that account in *my* name, or I'm going to have to bruise your pretty little face and burn down your restaurant!"

Shelly struggled to remain calm, to think about where to get help. She studied the man who now had a fistful of her hair and tried to analyze whether he would really do her arm, or if he was just bluffing. He was big, but he didn't seem particularly smart. The plan was fraught with problems. In a town as small as Jester, where everyone knew everyone, he'd be identified as a stranger and if she appeared at all uncomfortable with him, someone would notice. The bank manager. And Luke's office was only half a block away.

And she might have thought it through and come up with a solution if the other man hadn't reached into the playpen for the baby. She felt herself turn into a wild woman, like the Hulk bursting out of his shirt.

She screamed, elbowed the gut of the man who held her, and leaped at the other one, grabbing his arm and smashing her other fist into his face. As he doubled over in pain, she swept the baby up and ran for the front door, her heart pounding.

She was halfway to the door when the first man caught her by the hair and dragged her to a stop. She clutched the baby to her as the man leaned over her, his lip curled in anger.

But a large fist connected with his face and he flew backward with a cry of surprise and pain. She stared at Connor in shock.

Then he shoved her out of the way as the second man dove at him. As they struggled, she ran to call Luke, whose number she had on speed dial since she'd found the baby, and pleaded for him to hurry. Then she snatched the frying pan off the stove and returned with it raised for action.

"Max, Senior" had been struggling to his feet, but changed his mind when he saw her coming. He lay on his back, leaning heavily on one arm and raising the other hand in surrender.

Connor was just getting to his feet, the second man out cold near the door.

"What happened?" Connor asked breathlessly as he came toward her. The baby was screaming and he took Max from her, then wrapped an arm around Shelly's shoulders. "Are you hurt?"

She leaned into him, hardly able to believe he was there. It seemed to make everything in her world right again. She put her fingertips to his eye where a bruise was already forming. "I'm fine, but you're going to have a shiner." She pointed to the first man. "He claims to be Max's father, but he was just after Max's bank account. He wanted me to go to the bank with him and put it in his name."

Connor turned to the man with a look of hatred. "Max, Senior" raised both hands in surrender this time, and lay back as though to prove his intentions. "I'm done," he said. "I'm done."

Luke was there in two minutes. "Well, well," he said, looking from the second man, who was just regaining consciousness, to the first, who was now propped up on his elbows looking confused. "If it isn't the Yates brothers from Pine Run. Tried to work a scam on Shelly, did you?" he asked, his grinning glance bouncing off the frying pan in her hand. "Don't tell me you're into your bookie again."

The first man pointed to his brother. "Arch said it'd be easy," he explained, letting his arm drop to his propped knee in disgust. "Just a little woman and a baby. God!" He fixed Shelly with a look of injury. "You train with the Green Berets, or somethin'?"

"He tried to take the baby," Connor explained, "because of the bank account Shelly set up." He told him about the trip the man wanted her to make to the bank.

A sudden flash interrupted their conversation, and they all turned to the door to see Harvey Brinkman and his photographer.

"Did you get hurt, Shelly?" Harvey asked, taking a step inside. "Was there any attempt to...you know..." He waggled his eyebrows in a way she could only imagine suggested that the men had had illicit intentions as well as robbery on their mind.

Connor strode to the door. The photographer had already backed out of the room, but Connor put a hand to the middle of Harvey's chest and pushed him backward. "But she's the darling of Jester," Harvey was saying. "People will want to know..."

Connor gave him one final shove and closed the door.

Luke put one man, then the other in the cage in the back of his car. "I'll need to talk to you this afternoon, Shelly," he said, sticking his head in the door. "But I hear you took a tumble at the restaurant and came home to get some sleep. So you don't have to hurry. You okay?"

"Fine," she replied, going to the door. "I'll see you after lunch. Is that okay?"

"Fine. 'Bye. 'Bye, Doc."

"'Bye, Luke."

Connor shifted the now sniffling baby to his other arm and followed Shelly into the kitchen. "Tumble?"

She stopped at the refrigerator and shrugged. "I fell while delivering an order. I made a terrible mess, but didn't get hurt." She took a tissue from her pocket and dabbed at the baby's wet cheeks. "Dan sent me home. I own the place, but he has his bossy moments."

She was trembling inside, and she held the refrigerator door, hoping it didn't show in her hands. She couldn't imagine what was wrong with her.

Fear, of course, she thought as she opened the door and peered inside. Fear for the baby, fear for herself. The perfectly understandable fear at being closed in her house with two scary men and no rescue in sight.

Except that Connor had appeared out of nowhere. Connor, who thought she couldn't make her own decisions.

She waited for resentment over the things he'd said last night to overpower the sheer relief she'd felt at his arrival, the joy she couldn't help now as he stood just a few feet away, rocking the baby from side to side.

It didn't happen. She was just so glad to see him on several levels.

"So…" she asked, taking a container of stew out

of the freezer "…what brought you here in the first place?"

He patted Max's back as the baby leaned his head on his shoulder and yawned. "I was coming to pick up my stuff."

That was not at all the answer she'd hoped for. She pried the top off the container, set it back on again and put it in the microwave. "I haven't touched anything," she said with a polite smile, indicating his room. "You want a box or a bag?"

"I've changed my mind," he said.

She dug in a drawer for a wooden spoon. "Oh?" *Now* he would give her the answer she wanted.

"I hadn't thought about you and the baby being in danger from someone wanting your money. Or his money."

That wasn't the answer, either. But it occurred to her that it might serve for the moment if it would keep him here without her having to ask. Though she couldn't appear too eager. "Oh, we'll be fine," she said. "Once Harvey gets the photo of me brandishing the skillet in the paper, it'll serve as a warning to anyone else with the same intentions."

"I'm staying," he said. "When Mrs. Pearson picks up Max tomorrow, I'm out of your life."

Great. He was giving her nothing to work with, here. "It's a deal," she said. "You want some stew?"

He glanced at his watch. "It's not even ten o'clock."

She smiled at him, trying to look as uninvolved as

he sounded. "Are you one of those who eats only breakfast stuff for breakfast? No cold pizza, leftover Chinese food?"

He nodded. "I used to in medical school and during my residency when my life was upside down. But I've been trying to get myself better organized."

"Bacon and eggs, then?" she offered, opening the fridge again.

"No," he replied. "I'd love the stew."

She leaned her weight on one hip and closed the door. "Now that doesn't even make sense."

"I know." He started toward the living room with the baby, then stopped in the doorway to add over his shoulder, "Nothing about this relationship does, so why bother trying?"

The microwave dinged. She took the container out, broke up the thawing mass with the wooden spoon and put it back in again, smiling privately to herself. That was the most hopeful thing he'd said since he'd come to her rescue.

SHELLY'S HOME INVASION was the lead story on the ten-o'clock news from Helena, with Harvey Brinkman answering interview questions in his flack jacket and a Marlow-esque air. His article on the event appeared on the front page of the *Pine Run Plain Talker* and was picked up by most of the other Montana papers. And Shelly had been right. The photo that accompanied the story was of her wielding the frypan.

Connor noted that he and Luke were identified in

the caption but hardly mentioned in the story except to say that they'd arrived after Shelly had subdued the criminals.

Luke, sitting beside Connor at the Cup's counter the following noon, laughed at their apparent insignificance. "Darn women's movement," he said, downing the last of his coffee. "Makes it hard to be a hero anymore. You decked both of them and I hauled them away, and we get no credit at all. Though, according to Calvin Yates, she *was* fighting like a tiger."

Connor nodded. "Frying pan scared me."

"Me, too."

"What time's Mrs. Pearson coming?"

Luke shook his head. "I told Shelly just before you got here that Mrs. Pearson isn't coming till Friday. She's got the flu everybody else in her office had. They're all overworked catching up, so her cases have to wait."

Connor was happy to hear that. Shelly had been morose that morning and called him at the medical center to tell him that she was formally filing for custody and asked him to ask Nathan if he'd be prepared to back her up. He'd thought she seemed a little giddy this afternoon.

"You know Shelly intends to file for custody."

"She called me this morning."

"The news story should improve her chances, don't you think? She was determined that those guys weren't getting Max."

Luke smiled. "I think so."

"Good."

So Shelly could eventually adopt Max, Connor thought, and the two of them could live happily ever after while he tried to pretend it wasn't ripping his heart out to see them together.

Oh, hell. He'd endured heartbreak before.

This was different, though, he realized. With Lisa, he'd only thought he'd been in love. With Shelly, there was no doubt.

Shelly came out of the kitchen with two giant hot-fudge sundaes and placed one in front of each of them.

Luke blinked. "I didn't order this," he said.

"I know." She pushed it closer to him. "It's hot-fudge sundae day. A sort of customer-appreciation thing I'm doing. Everyone gets a free one with lunch."

"Ah…" Luke seemed prepared to demur, but she pushed it back at him.

"Eat it," she said firmly, "or I'll hit you with my frying pan."

Amanda, on the other side of Luke, shook her head at Shelly. "Money's made you such a savage. Where's mine?"

Shelly rolled her eyes at her. "Wait your turn. I've only got two hands."

"Well, you'd think with all that money," Amanda called after her, "you'd be able to buy another one!"

Chapter Eleven

"How would you feel about going to Pine Run tomorrow?" Shelly asked Connor that night over dinner. They sat on opposite sides of a red-and-white-checked tablecloth spread out on the living-room floor, a continuation, she'd explained, of the day's celebration. Sean Connery, who'd disappeared during the melee with the Yates brothers, was perched on the edge of the cloth.

"An extension of customer-appreciation day?" he'd teased. "Since we're at home, just what kind of customer am I? And what kind of business are you running?"

She made a face at his suggestion. "It's just a continuation of the celebration, and at this point it has no name. We're just partying. I had a red-and-white tablecloth, a bottle of Chianti and spaghetti in the freezer. It was serendipitous. Or whatever that is in Italian."

"Ah. Well, then. I'm delighted to be a part of it."

And he was. There was a curious peace between

them that lacked the sparkle that had existed between them before. But it also lacked the heartache of their separation, so he was happy enough with it.

"When Nathan returned my call this afternoon, he told me you were off tomorrow. And he's willing to come to court for me, by the way."

"Right on both counts," Connor replied, reaching to the middle of the tablecloth for a bread stick. "Weather's a little quieter. Should be easy driving. But is there any particular reason?"

"Yes." She batted her eyelashes. It was a playful gesture, but it surprised him. She was almost openly flirtatious. He wasn't sure what to make of it. "I'm going to buy clothes and makeup. There's a little outlet mall there that has everything I need. Your job, I'm afraid, is to keep Max happy and be a sort of fashion critic."

He winced. "Fashion critic?"

"You lived in L.A. just recently," she said. "You should know what's trendy."

"I never paid much attention."

She dismissed that claim with a swing of her bread stick. "You know how to make love in a bathtub. Don't tell me you never noticed women."

Okay. He was going to have to give her some of her own back. She couldn't torture him like this and not expect retribution. "You instinctively *knew* how to make love in a bathtub. If you consider that a measurement of fashion sense—though I can't say I make the connection—then you're qualified yourself. Maybe even overqualified.''

Her eyes met his without flinching. His blood pressure rose and his rapid pulse was rattling his arm.

''I'm sorry about the fight,'' she said, dropping her bread stick on her plate.

That was easy enough to agree with. ''So am I.''

''Maybe we could just agree to disagree on the subject of marriage.'' She sounded hopeful.

He would have liked to agree to that, too, but simply couldn't give up the fight.

''I'll just disagree, if you don't mind,'' he said. ''On principle.''

She shook her head at him. ''The principle that you have to have it your way?''

''The principle,'' he corrected, ''that we'd be very happy loving each other forever.''

''I'm offering you that.''

''No,'' he said patiently, ''you're not. You're inviting me to stay with you, not to marry you.''

''Why isn't that enough?''

He wanted to hold it back, knowing it would result in the same old argument all over again. But she was waiting for an answer. ''Because, for the way I want to live, it isn't adult enough for me. You're so used to living your parents' life, that you're afraid to live your own. And you know if you promise yourself to me, that's what it would mean. A step out into your own life.''

She got to her feet with a growl. ''And I think,''

she said, obviously fighting temper, "that you want to…to mortar me into place so that I don't leave like Lisa did."

He stood also, shaken by her perception of what he offered. "Is that how you think marriage would be—like two bricks held together with mortar?" He jammed his hands in his pockets and took a few steps away, then turned and came back. "I was thinking in terms of something less cold and rigid. Like two flowers in a vase. Two books on a shelf. Each with its own identity, but together."

Her eyes brimmed with tears, and she said with a determined toss of her head, "I am free for the first time in my life. And that's the way I want it." She took several steps toward him, just a few steps separating them. "I'd love to have you here with me, but I have been so confined all my life, I can't promise that again."

He spread his hands helplessly. "Then, I guess that's it. I'll keep Max happy tomorrow so you can do your shopping, and I'll even stretch my abilities to be your fashion consultant. But when Mrs. Pearson comes, I'm out of here."

There was a defeated inclination of her head, then she nodded. "I understand," she said.

He reached for Max's carrier. "I'll give him his bottle. I may as well take advantage of my last few opportunities to spend time with him."

"Sure," she said, busying herself with gathering up the remnants of their picnic.

CONNOR EXPECTED the shopping trip to be a disaster, but, again, they'd found a curiously companionable level on which to coexist without actually sharing their lives as they'd done before. She seemed willing to hold no grudges and he certainly believed she'd given him far more good than bad in the time they'd spent together.

So he followed her from shop to shop, the baby happy and bright-eyed and crying only when hungry or sleepy.

It was almost enjoyable in the beginning to watch her try on clothes, do a turn in front of the three-way mirror that seemed to populate the world with dozens of her. She was slender and graceful and surprisingly stunning when free of the pants, sweaters and aprons she always wore.

In one shop she tried on a flared and sequined black dress with a pair of black heels with almost nothing to hold them on but two tiny straps. She smoothed the neckline, then the waist, and did a turn toward him that flared the skirt and made it sparkle.

"What do you think?" she asked. She looked excited. He was sure she was seeing something in herself she'd probably never had time to notice before. She was beautiful, and for the first time in her life she had time to explore where that could take her. She didn't have to work like a dog if she didn't want to. She could do all the things she'd always wanted to do, and she didn't have to do them alone. She had Max.

"I think you and the dress are gorgeous," he replied honestly. And that was the last coherent thought he managed before he sank into a well of misery.

It had been one thing to argue with her about what he thought best for them, but quite another to realize, like a sudden epiphany, that what was best for him probably wasn't best for her at this point in time.

For the first time since they'd started to argue about this, he really understood that he'd lost.

He wasn't sure how he survived the next two hours. The lingerie was particularly difficult. The clerk helping her, not realizing they weren't a family, swept aside the curtain on her dressing room in line with the chair on which he and a sleeping Max waited. Shelly looked embarrassed, then shrugged in an "Oh, well" gesture and struck a pose for him.

She wore a one-piece thing in pink silk that clung to her pert breasts and draped loosely over her hips, except that when she moved, the fabric clung and outlined her curves.

He was too far away for them to hear his groan as he gave her a thumbs-up.

Despite his objections, she bought him a tie with tools all over it, a dressy tweed jacket she'd caught him admiring and a box of chocolates.

"Shelly," he said firmly. "I'm not even wild about chocolates."

She smiled at him. "That's why I'm going to help you eat them."

"Why didn't you just buy them for yourself?"

"Because that would be indulgent."

Sure. He didn't have to make sense of things, he just had to survive the day.

She bought makeup, and several clips and things for her hair and all kinds of things for the baby.

It was dark when they headed home, and he drove carefully, aware of the dangers of the snowy roads. Mercifully, the baby was asleep, and Shelly lay back drowsily, unusually quiet for her. He found himself yearning for the sound of her voice.

"Warm enough?" he asked.

"Yes, thanks," she replied.

"Where are you going to wear the black dress?"

"Tuscany," she said without hesitation.

He glanced at her quickly. "Really. I didn't know you wanted to go there."

"You can take a culinary tour of the area," she said with a dreamy sigh, "eating *and* cooking. I'd love to do that. I'm sure there must be some wonderful restaurant or hotel where I can wear my dress."

"Right."

"You could come with me, you know," she said wistfully.

He didn't want to get into that again. "Some of us have to work for a living," he teased.

"I thought you had more disposable income than I do."

"I do. But when I came to work for Nathan, I promised to be available pretty much all the time for the first year. He's desperate for a break, and I can relate to that. I'm going to have to get my kicks out of finding a house to buy while you're sparkling in Tuscany.''

She sighed. "Too bad."

"Yeah," he said.

Chapter Twelve

It was just after two in the morning when Shelly put her bedside lamp on and padded quietly to the closet to get the sequined dress she'd hung there. Then she went to peer into Max's crib. In the shadowy corner of the room, he remained fast asleep.

She lay the dress on her bed and sat cross-legged beside it, trying to imagine herself in it in among the olive groves on a moonlit night in some northwestern Italian hideaway.

She got the picture, then tried to imagine her excitement at being there. But that wouldn't quite come. She saw herself, one side of her hair clipped back with the tiny silver butterfly she'd bought, her dress glittering in the moonlight, the high heels dangling from her fingers as she leaned over a flowered balcony to look down at the olive trees below.

But she couldn't feel what that woman felt. It was as though that woman wasn't her.

She folded her arms in disgust. This was just some weird self-deprivation thing going on in her mind because she was trying to think about exploring life beyond Jester. It would be so good for her. Good for Max.

She hung the dress up again and glanced at the clock—2:07 a.m. She was getting to be as bad as the baby, she thought with bleak humor. She hadn't closed her eyes once tonight, and as the Fates would have it, Max slept on contentedly.

She was too restless to lie down again, and too fidgety to find something to do. But her mind kept conjuring up images of Connor and she didn't want to think about him now. Memories of making love with him flashed vividly behind her eyes and she struggled to ignore how much being with him meant to her.

How much it had changed her.

She used to be a woman of purpose and direction, but now felt as though every step she took was in darkness. She used to want nothing more than to stay in Jester, run the restaurant that was a legacy from her parents and be a friend to her friends. She'd accepted that the exciting relationships other women enjoyed were not for her.

Then she'd won the lottery and suddenly dozens of opportunities she'd once thought would never come her way now lay open to her. The possibilities were exciting. She could travel, see and do all the things she'd once thought impossible. But now she was confused. Stay or go? Love or learn?

Then fate gave her a baby and a man on the same day. If she'd thought she was confused before, that was nothing to the chaotic thoughts she now suffered. Keep the baby? Love the man? Keep the restaurant? Take a trip? There seemed no way possible to accommodate all four issues at the same time.

She turned off the light and went back to bed, her mind in a whirl. She really should try to get some sleep. She had to be up early tomorrow. Betsy wouldn't have thought to reset the tables for the morning. And the soup had to be prepared.

She fell back against her pillows and wondered why life always had to be so complicated. Why couldn't she have just fallen in love with a man, taken a trip, had a baby, then won the lottery? Timing, it was said, was everything.

She turned onto her side and snuggled into her pillow, wishing desperately that it was Connor. Then she heard a noise.

It was a very small sound. A clink of something. The garbage can against the side of the house? Raccoons, maybe. She lay still and listened.

She heard something again, but this had a slightly different tone. Not high like a clink, but soft yet shuddering.

Like the opening of a window!

No, that couldn't be. She kept all her windows locked. She sat up abruptly, her heart hammering, as she remembered that this morning she'd unlocked the window over the kitchen sink to check the state of the bird feeder outside. Had she locked it again? She couldn't remember.

Then there was a loud thud, a cry of alarm in a high, female voice, then a shouted order. That was Connor's voice.

Shelly grabbed her robe, left the door open so she could hear the baby and flew down the stairs. She was shocked to find Connor, still dressed as he'd been all day, with a firm grip on the arm of what looked like a high school girl.

A high school girl who appeared to be having a major meltdown. She was very small, with one disheveled dark brown braid, her blue eyes filled with despair. She was sobbing hysterically.

"What happened?" Shelly asked Connor as she approached them.

"She broke in through the window," he said in consternation. "I caught her heading for the stairs."

To Shelly's complete and utter shock, the girl broke away from Connor and flew into her arms.

"Oh, please!" she wept, holding Shelly tightly. "Please. I didn't want to leave him, but I didn't have a car or a place to live or money to buy diapers. I didn't know what to do! And I remembered that you'd been nice to me."

I didn't want to leave him. Shelly held the fragile young woman away from her and looked into her eyes. She saw Max in her eyes and her nose. And caught a whiff of the subtle rose scent that had clung to Max when she'd found him in her restaurant.

A crushing, painful weight descended on her chest.

"I'm Max's mother," the girl whispered, swiping

a hand across her eyes in an effort to stop crying. But her eyes spilled tears again and she continued to sob. "I'm so sorry. I know I'm awful! I just didn't know what to do."

Shelly looked up at Connor. She was sure her eyes were filled with the grim dread she felt. He looked as though he shared her anguish.

But he couldn't help her. No one could help her.

Max's mother was back.

He pushed them both gently toward the sofa. "Do you want me to call Luke?" he asked Shelly.

The girl put a trembling hand to her mouth. "Luke. That's the sheriff, isn't it? I saw him in the paper."

"Yes," Shelly replied a little sharply. "You just broke into my home, young lady. How old are you?"

That was it, she thought with a tiny swell of hope. The girl had abandoned her baby, then broken into Shelly's home. Certainly those were two crimes that could be used against her when Shelly filed for custody.

"I'm nineteen," the girl said, swiping again at her tear-streaked face. "My friend and her mom said I could stay with them in Pine Run, and I can have the baby there. I just have to find a job. Please let me take him home with me!"

"Where are your parents?"

"My dad died when I was twelve, and my mom married this guy who was always trying to…" She hesitated, then looked her in the eye and said with a shake of her head, "We just didn't get along."

Shelly winced at the realization of what the girl really meant but didn't say.

"I left when I was sixteen and I did pretty well. There was a shelter in Oregon where I stayed for a long time. I liked it there. But you have to leave when you're eighteen, but that was okay because I had a good job as a waitress in a classy place on the river. Then I met Max's father." She sighed heavily, and said in a sad and sincerely adult tone, "If I'd known then what I know now... He had big plans to open a motorcycle repair shop, but it never happened. I ended up supporting him *and* me."

"Why didn't you just knock on the door?" Connor asked. "And try to explain all this? Why break in?"

She turned to him with a world-weary look. "Because I knew you wouldn't let me in. You'd think I was just another stupid girl who got pregnant then decided she didn't like having a baby after all."

"You're not?" he asked mercilessly.

"I was," she admitted candidly after a moment. "I thought I knew everything. I thought I knew Max's father. I thought he meant it when he said he loved me, that he didn't mean it when he said he didn't want a baby, and I thought when he saw our beautiful Max he'd come back." Tears streamed down her pale, peaked face. "I think he's surfing somewhere in Mexico." She sniffed. Shelly offered her a box of tissues and she took one. "Thank you. Things got so bad before that I...I panicked. It wasn't that I wanted time to party or anything, it was just that I didn't have any money, and I couldn't get a job and take care of Max, too, so I left him at the coffee shop. I'd read the article about how all you Main Street Millionaires just got your money." The girl smiled shakily. "You don't remember me, do you?"

Shelly studied the big-eyed little face but couldn't honestly say that she did.

"I'm Valerie Simms. I came to town looking for work when I left with Max's father. I was waiting for the truck to pick me up and I didn't have money for breakfast. But I bought a small orange juice. You asked me if I wanted something to go with it, and when I told you I didn't have the money, you made me pancakes and bacon. I never forgot that."

Shelly only vaguely remembered the incident. She often fed someone she thought was in need. She thought of it as her pro bono work.

"I'll make some coffee," Connor said, going toward the kitchen. "We can call Luke later."

The girl watched him walk away. "The paper said he's the new doctor and that he's your boyfriend."

"He is the new doctor," Shelly said. "He's been helping me with Max."

"He doesn't like me."

"He loves Max," she explained. "And he comes from a big city where a lot of babies are abused and neglected. He doesn't like it when mothers mistreat their children."

The girl looked up at her and Shelly could see in her eyes that she'd been plagued by guilt since she'd left Max on the Cup's counter. "I thought I was doing the right thing for him."

"The right thing," Shelly said gently, "if you were sure you had to give him up, would have been to take him to a CFS office."

"I didn't want just anyone to get him," she said. "I wanted *you* to have him."

"I was going to tell the caseworker tomorrow that I want to adopt him," Shelly said.

The girl caught her hands and when tears would have threatened again, she fought them off with a brave intake of breath. "I want him back, Miss Dupree," she said, her eyes pleading. "I know what I did was awful, but this time without him has proved to me that whatever happens, Max and I are a family and I can't live without him. I've been miserable."

"He's been comfortable and happy," Shelly said, trying to be heartless, certain she was better for Max than this girl could ever be. "I think you have to consider what's best for him, rather than what's best for you."

"I know that's true," Valerie said. Shelly saw in her expressive eyes that she did. "But he's mine! I was scared a week ago, but now I know I can raise my baby. I have job applications out all over. It's just that now that Christmas is over, nobody needs extra help. But I'm going to find something."

Connor appeared with three mugs of coffee.

"Have you eaten?" Shelly asked Valerie.

Valerie nodded. "I'm fine." She looked miserable.

"I read about what you did in the paper. About the guys who wanted to take Max because you opened a bank account for him." She frowned suddenly. "You probably think that's why I'm here. Because of the bank account."

Shelly wished she could say with righteous indignation that she did, but she didn't. The girl's anguish was too real. "No, I don't," she said.

Valerie turned to Connor, who sat in the chair opposite the sofa. "I'll bet you do," she accused quietly.

"It's hard for me to know what to think of you," he said reasonably. "You abandoned your baby, then you broke into Shelly's house. It's hard to have good thoughts about someone who'd do either of those things. On the other hand, it sounds as though you've had a difficult time. And when you explain the reasons behind what you did…" He drew a breath and sipped at his coffee. "I don't know," he said finally. "I guess it all depends on whether or not you're telling the truth. And we won't know that until Luke checks it out for us in the morning."

She looked as though she'd lost her lifeline. But she nodded. "Do you think I could see Max before I go?"

Shelly couldn't imagine depriving her of the sight of her son. "Yes. Come with me." She brought her up to the bedroom where Max slept like an angel.

"He didn't sleep very well for me," Valerie whispered, tears literally raining down her face as she put a hand gently on Max's tummy. "He was fussy most of the time."

Shelly nodded. "We've been up with him a lot. He's just beginning to settle down a little."

"He's so beautiful!"

"Yes."

Valerie looked around at the little bit of the room visible in the light from the hallway. Then she turned back to her son, her eyes wild with pain. "I'm not sure I could ever give him a house like this."

All kinds of responses leaped to Shelly's tongue. She was as surprised as Valerie when the words that came out were empathetic. "He doesn't need a particular kind of house, Valerie. Just a particular kind of mother. One who'll love him no matter what."

Valerie hurried out of the room and down the stairs. Shelly stood alone in the hallway, contemplating her options. She hated all of them.

She could try to fight for Max and possibly win at least temporary custody until Valerie had a chance to prove more adult behavior to the court.

Or she could admit to herself that Valerie had done the best she could in a very difficult life and that when it came to the crunch, she'd given her baby to a woman she knew was kind—an action anyone would be hard-pressed to criticize.

And—hell—she could take the high road and do what she could to help this girl who really needed a break. Maybe even deserved one.

Connor and Valerie stood side by side, Connor's

size dwarfing the girl's petite stature. He had a hand to her shoulder, in comfort this time, Shelly guessed.

"...tough, I know," he was saying, "but sometimes you just have to own up to a bad decision and deal with the results as gracefully as you can. How you handle it will make a difference the next time you're faced with a problem."

Valerie nodded and wrapped her thin jacket more tightly around herself. "What time should I be back to talk to the sheriff?" she asked. "I promise I'll come."

"It's so late," Shelly replied. It wasn't what she'd intended to say, it just came out. "You can stay the night here, then we'll talk to the sheriff in the morning. The caseworker from Pine Run is due also. So we can talk to her about Max."

Valerie stared at Shelly in disbelief. "You mean... stay here?" she asked after a moment.

"It's just a bed," Shelly said. "Maybe breakfast. And Max stays in my room."

The girl continued to stare, then nodded.

"Go on up. Take the room at the top of the stairs. Do you have to call your friend's mom or anyone?"

Valerie shook her head. "They work nights at a janitorial company. I'll call in the morning and tell them I'm here."

"Okay. See you in the morning."

With one last confused look at Shelly, Valerie climbed the stairs.

"What are you doing?" Connor asked the moment the girl was out of earshot.

Her momentary courage and nobility gone, Shelly turned to him, her faced crumpling, her arms reaching blindly for him.

He swore softly and took her into his embrace. "Shelly, she's probably a sweet kid," he said quietly, "but she abandoned her baby. *You* deserve Max. Max deserves *you*. Don't go getting unnecessarily noble because her regrets break your heart."

She didn't have the breath or the will to argue with him. "Please come up with me," she said.

He swept her up in his arms without answering and carried her to her room. She went to the crib and stood over it for a long moment, pain visible in every line of her body. Then she climbed into bed with her robe still on, and he kicked off his shoes and followed. She curled into him and wrapped her arm around his waist. She wept until the alarm rang at five o'clock.

She climbed out of bed with a calm Connor found a little unsettling.

"I have to go open the restaurant," she said, "and see if I can get Betsy to come in and cover for me again. If you want to come with me," Shelly told Valerie, who stood uncertainly in the middle of the hallway, "I'll get you some breakfast, and you can call your friend's mother so she doesn't worry about you."

"Okay," Valerie said.

Shelly turned to Connor. "You coming, too?"

He couldn't determine whether she wanted his company, or if she needed time alone with Valerie. He was sure that she was in a dangerous mood this morning. She was courteous, even smiled, but it was as though she'd built a wall around herself as something indeterminate went on in her mind. Even Valerie seemed to notice and was watching her worriedly.

"I'm coming," he replied. "Give me ten minutes. I'll shower downstairs."

A little cry came from the crib in Shelly's bedroom. Valerie's eyes darted to it and she took a step toward it, but stopped when Shelly went into the bedroom. Connor grudgingly gave Valerie credit for deferring to her.

Shelly carried a very bright-eyed Max out of the bedroom. Apparently unable to help herself, Valerie went to them.

"Hi, Maxie," Valerie said softly, her voice thick with tears. "Hi, baby."

Max looked at her with no more interest than he would have another stranger.

She put a hand up to him and he caught her index finger and brought it to his mouth. Tears slid down her cheeks.

Shelly tried to put him in Valerie's arms, but he fussed and reached for Shelly.

"It's okay," Valerie said with a painful sniff. "He doesn't remember me. I...I didn't think that would happen so fast."

"He has a bottle in the refrigerator," Shelly said,

rocking him from side to side. "I bet he'll let you give it to him while I shower."

Valerie walked dejectedly down the stairs to retrieve it.

"You're not leaving her alone with him," Connor challenged.

"You'll be here," she said, going back into the bedroom with him, pulling a few things out of her closet.

Connor thought the next half hour was like watching scenes in a movie. The little life he and Shelly and Max had shared, though fraught with his disagreements with Shelly, had seemed real and affecting. He'd once imagined the three of them being together forever and it had felt right.

Then they'd decided it wouldn't work after all. But now he was here and she seemed to appreciate that. Would she change her mind about marrying him now if she was going to fight for custody? Or did she intend to do something that might mean she wouldn't need him at all?

It was impossible to tell by her quiet, unrevealing face.

With his bottle for comfort, Max was willing to let Valerie hold him. He looked up at her with interest and maybe even some kind of tiny baby memory of the past. His little fingers opened and closed on the bottle as he drank greedily and studied her.

Unable to watch any longer, Connor went to sit on the top stair, pain wrenching at his gut.

He heard Shelly come out of the shower. "Your turn," he heard her say to Valerie. "I know you don't have a change of clothes, but I can lend you a sweater. It won't matter if it's too big."

When he heard the bathroom door close behind Valerie, he went downstairs to get himself ready for what he guessed was bound to be a difficult day.

They were a little late arriving at the Cup, and a few of the regulars were already there, sitting at the counter with their cups, watching the coffee drip.

Shelly handed Valerie the baby and pointed her to the playpen in the corner. "He spends a lot of the day there, getting attention from everyone who comes and goes."

Dan raised an eyebrow at Connor at the sight of Valerie. "The mother?" he asked under his breath.

"So she claims," Connor replied.

Dan swore.

"Yeah," Connor concurred, and waited with everyone else for a cup of coffee while Shelly called Betsy.

The pot was finally full and he was about to walk around the counter and get it when Valerie appeared, tying on an apron and reaching for the pot. She poured cups for Dean and his cronies, who studied her interestedly. Irene had come in and was crooning at Max.

"New waitress?" Dean asked.

Valerie smiled. "For this morning, anyway."

"We usually sit in the back booth."

She nodded. "Go ahead. I'll just pour Connor's coffee, find an order pad and be right back there."

Connor pointed to the cubbyhole under the cash register where he'd seen Shelly put her pads.

Valerie pulled one out, studied it a moment then took a quick look at a menu tucked behind the napkin holder. She drew a breath and headed for Dean's booth.

Shelly hurried out of the back, shrugging into her cobbler apron, and stopped in surprise at the sight of Valerie waiting on Dean's booth.

"You put her to work?" she asked Connor.

"No," he replied. "She took it upon herself. You get covered for today?"

"Yes. But she can't be here for another hour."

"Did you call Luke?"

She glanced at the clock. "He doesn't answer, but he'll probably be in for breakfast in half an hour. What would you like to eat?"

He caught her hand as she would have reached for the coffeepot to refill the cup he'd already drained.

"Shelly, what are you going to do?" he asked. She seemed as though she existed somewhere beyond his reach, and even though he had a hold of her wrist, he really hadn't made contact.

She looked into his eyes, expelled a breath, and he knew she'd come back from wherever she'd retreated to to prepare for the day.

"I honestly don't know."

"You want to talk about it?"

Even as Connor asked the question, the coffee shop door opened and two burly men in coveralls walked in, followed by Jack Hartman and two women he didn't know.

Shelly indicated them with a tilt of her head. "Who has time to talk? Pancakes and bacon before the rush is on?"

He drew his hand back and held out his cup, resigned to being left in the dark. "Sure."

After breakfast, he stepped outside to call Nathan at home and explain what had happened. He promised to take weekend call if Nathan would cover him today.

"Of course," Nathan said. "Shelly still planning to file for custody?"

"I don't know," Connor replied. "But I'll keep you posted."

"Please do. And remember that she'll love you best for letting her do what she wants to do."

"Even if it's wrong?"

"If she wants to do it, she won't think it's wrong. And sometimes when you're determined to do something, you can make it turn out right."

"Paymaster *and* philosopher. Thanks, Nathan."

"Sure. See you."

LUKE WAS LATE for breakfast.

Shelly looked worriedly at the clock, but she didn't have time to speculate on what was keeping him, when Harvey Brinkman walked in with his photographer.

"Relax, doll," he said, when she fixed him with a threatening look, a plate of scrambled eggs in one hand and sausage and biscuits in the other. "I'm just here to do a story about your projects board." He pointed to the board Jack had mounted for her near the door.

She looked at it in some surprise. She'd been so deep in her own thoughts the past few days that she'd failed to notice how many of the townspeople had weighed in on what projects they wanted tackled first. Connor, who'd been reading the paper in the back booth, waiting for Luke's arrival, started to get up as though ready to intervene.

She stayed him with a raised hand.

"All right," she said grudgingly to Harvey. "Sit down and I'll bring you some coffee."

His photographer took a long shot of the board, then an up-close shot of the top contenders for immediate action. Harvey copied the list, then noted a few of the comments voters had tacked on to their decisions.

"Looks like the church roof's got it," Harvey said as she brought two cups of coffee to the first booth where he had tossed his jacket. He leaned in to read one of the comments. "'So it doesn't rain in on our Valentine vows.'" He turned to her. "What's that?" the photographer asked.

"Every Valentine's Day," she explained after delivering her order, "married couples promise to keep loving each other. Engaged couples, and those just in love, promise to keep trying to understand each other and give to each other. Anyone who wants to come is welcome. Then there's a dance in the church hall."

"Cute," he said.

She groaned privately and cleared a table. Cute. Only someone who'd never loved anybody could think that the daily effort to understand and choose to love was "cute."

And then it hit her, like one of the overhead lights falling on her head. She *knew* what love was about! She felt it for Connor. He loved her! Well, he had once.

But she was trying to hold on to her cute little life because—God! Connor was right!—marriage would make her a grown-up. And so far, all she'd ever been to anyone, even years after their deaths, was her parents' daughter. And that was no one's fault but her own.

The front door opened, and Luke walked in with Louise Pearson. Shelly's heart thumped in her chest. She'd hoped to have had time to talk to him before Mrs. Pearson arrived. And she hadn't wanted to be in the middle of a personal revelation.

She forced herself back to the moment. She met them near the counter, reaching out to shake Mrs. Pearson's hand.

The woman looked concerned. "Where's Max?" she asked.

Shelly pointed to the playpen where the baby was holding court with Jack Hartman and Amanda Bradley.

"I see he's completely recovered," she observed.

"He's doing beautifully," Connor said, appearing at Shelly's side.

Shelly couldn't tell if Mrs. Pearson was pleased to see the baby so happily ensconced in the restaurant or not.

Shelly drew her toward the playpen. His wide smile revealed the two bottom teeth had broken through, two ragged little shiny white buds.

The woman finally smiled.

"And how are you?" Shelly asked politely. "I hear you've been ill."

She nodded briskly. "But I'm fine now. And we have to decide what to do about this baby. The sheriff tells me you'd like to file for custody."

Shelly looked up, saw that Valerie stood frozen near the counter. Betsy was still pouring coffee and taking orders.

She pointed through the kitchen. "Would you like to talk in my office?"

The woman nodded perfunctorily. "Of course."

"Can I get you a cup of coffee?"

"Please."

At her raised eyebrow, Luke nodded. "Me, too, please."

She set up a fresh pot for Betsy, hooked her finger in half a dozen cups and grabbed the full pot. Valerie scooped Max out of the playpen. For one pregnant moment, Shelly wondered if she'd made a terrible mistake. Valerie glanced at the door, apparently considering the possibility of escape with her baby.

Connor had grabbed several chairs from one of the empty tables and had carried them into the office, out of sight. Shelly's hands were full, so it would be hard for her to respond quickly if Valerie chose to run. The opportunity was tailor-made.

Valerie looked into Shelly's eyes, her thoughts clearly readable. Her eyes brimming, she turned in the direction of the office.

Shelly made everyone as comfortable as possible in the small space. She poured coffee for them and made introductions.

"Mrs. Pearson, Luke," she said, "I'd like you to meet Valerie Simms, Max's mother." Luke put his cup down on the edge of Shelly's desk, and the caseworker blinked in surprise.

"I thought you didn't know who she was," she said.

"I didn't," Shelly replied. "She came to my home last night to introduce herself and reclaim her son."

She saw Valerie's quick glance of gratitude at her sanitized recounting of events.

Mrs. Pearson lowered her cup to her lap and said, "Well, I'm afraid it won't be that simple. You were seriously neglectful of your baby, Miss Simms, and the law requires that certain procedures be followed. We—"

"Mrs. Pearson," Shelly interrupted, a sudden, brilliant inspiration taking shape inside her. She hated it, but it *was* brilliant.

Then she realized with a sudden, violent release of

pressure, that the only thing that created a sense of loss was a determination to have things or people in a way fate had determined they should not be. And if that was gone, everything simply...*was,* free to come and go where it would. Love could attract someone or something, but it couldn't lock it up.

Stunned by that realization, she stammered. "Um...ah...would you excuse Connor and me for just a minute? Maybe this would be a good time for Valerie to tell you what brought her to the point where she left Max with me, and how she feels about that now."

"Miss Dupree, I..."

"We'll just be a minute. I promise!"

Luke studied them worriedly. "Shelly, what...?"

"Just one minute," Shelly promised again. She turned to Connor. "Could I see you outside, please?"

When he hesitated, apparently as confused by her behavior as everyone else, she grabbed his wrist and pulled him with her out the door. Dan was working like a machine in the kitchen, and Betsy seemed to have things under control, though she was operating at top speed.

Shelly pulled Connor into the bathroom, the only private place available, and closed the door. She flipped on the light to reveal the tiny, very old cubicle with its spotless porcelain fixtures and wallpaper patterned with Victorian women in evening dress.

She saw Connor take a quick glance around him in surprise.

Looking up into his face, she realized that her new, wonderfully free philosophy was going to be hard to apply in this case. If Connor didn't concur with her plan, she didn't know what she'd do.

She had no time for subtlety.

"Will you marry me?" she asked.

"What?" He frowned and folded his arms. "Why?"

"Why?" she repeated, trying not to panic. "That's not an answer. Yes or no?"

"No," he said.

She stared at him in disbelief. She knew, of course, that they'd argued this over and over—always on different sides than they were taking now—but she'd lived in hope that when the moment came that she could believe that getting married was a good thing, he'd still be willing.

But he wasn't. It felt as though life stalled in her body.

"You said," she accused in a fractured voice, "that you love me."

"I do," he said without hesitation. "You're the one who doesn't love me."

She gasped in exasperation. "Yes, I do. I understand that now."

"Yeah, well, you'll have to explain it to me so that I understand it."

"Connor," she said, taking hold of his arms, "we don't have time for this. I need to know that you're with me on this."

"On what? Marriage?"

She blew out air that fluttered her bangs. "No. I need to know how you'd feel about sharing the house with a baby and a teenager."

He was afraid to admit even to himself how completely confused he could become when dealing with her. He knew he'd be able to understand this if he simply made an effort to follow along. Following wasn't usually his style, but he'd just been proposed to, and though he hadn't a clue why, he couldn't just let that slip away until he could get the offer on his terms.

"Max and…Valerie?"

"Yes," she said. Fluttering her fingertips in a hurry-up gesture. "What do you think? I'm sure our minute's up."

"You're inviting me to live with you?"

"No, I'm inviting you to marry me, but since you're being so difficult about it…"

"With Valerie and the baby."

"Yes."

Now he suspected what she was up to. He was both in awe of her courage to attempt it, and aware of the pain she must be feeling. Because he felt it, too. And though he wasn't going to settle for less than he wanted, he was so in love with her at this moment, he didn't know what to do with himself. And if he'd ever held doubts about her ability to make her own decisions, they were now resolved.

"I have no problem with that," he said.

She blinked, looking confused, too. That gave him a certain satisfaction.

"You don't?" She sounded surprised.

"No."

"And you'll back me up?"

He didn't want to admit this when he still needed some concessions from her, but she looked desperate. "Always," he replied.

She dropped her head to his shoulder for an instant, then caught his hand and led him back into the room.

Valerie was sobbing and Luke, who didn't look entirely comfortable with the job, was trying to quiet the screaming baby.

"I know it hurts, Valerie," Mrs. Pearson was saying with what appeared to be sincere but stern sympathy, "but you now have to prove your ability to raise your baby before I can place him back in your care. It's wonderful that you're living with a friend's mother, but we have to know that you'll be able to support your baby. We have to create a plan together and take it before a judge. And until we can do that, we have to know that Max will be safe."

Shelly took the baby from Luke, got the pacifier from her apron pocket and dipped it quickly in her coffee to sterilize it then wiped it off with a tissue and put it in Max's mouth. He quieted as though someone had turned him off and rested his head on her shoulder.

Luke sat down in relief. Connor resumed his chair

and Shelly sat down, as well, smiling at the case-worker.

"Mrs. Pearson," she said. "I have an idea."

The woman nodded wearily. "I'm always open to ideas."

"What if Max and Valerie both stayed with Connor and me?"

Valerie looked up in the middle of a sob, silenced just like the baby had been.

"Max has been very happy with us, and I think Valerie's sincere in wanting to be a good mother. She has experience as a waitress, and I could really use more regular help at the restaurant. I have a room for her and the baby, and I can keep an eye on them until the court date, and can report on how she and Max are doing together. The church has a weekly meeting of young mothers where they talk over solutions to problems and share what they're learning. That could help her, too."

Louise Pearson looked Shelly in the eye. "You're suggesting she stay with you?"

"Yes."

"You're assigning yourself a very big job."

Shelly shrugged. "Life's full of big jobs."

"Shelly!" Valerie whispered.

Shelly stood to put the now sleeping baby in his mother's arms.

Connor saw the wrenching pain she felt as she put aside the happy ending she'd wanted, to give Valerie the second chance that would probably change her life. He didn't think he'd ever seen such a selfless deed.

"Our goal," Mrs. Pearson said gently, as though afraid Shelly hadn't grasped it, "is to make Valerie self-sufficient."

Shelly nodded. "I understand that. And I know the difference between being Max's mother, and being Max's mother's friend. I've accepted it in my heart. We can do this, Mrs. Pearson."

Mrs. Pearson turned to Valerie. "Miss Dupree is willing to extend herself for you and the baby," she said, her tone quiet but her eyes firm. "Do *you* think you can do this? Keep a job and care for your baby?"

Valerie looked around at all the faces watching her, as though unable to believe what she'd heard. "Yes, I can," she said finally, and with a confidence Mrs. Pearson seemed to appreciate. "I promise I can."

"Well." Mrs. Pearson considered everyone involved, then got to her feet and glanced at her watch. "Valerie and I need to talk," she said. "Is there a private booth where we can have lunch and discuss a few things?"

"Of course." Shelly stood, also. "We'll find a booth for you and lunch is on me."

"No, no," Mrs. Pearson insisted. "I'm on an expense account." She beckoned to Valerie. "Come along, dear. Bring the baby."

Shelly led them out into the restaurant to find a booth.

Luke stood, tossing his hat in his hand. He looked

at Connor and drew a breath. "That was a solution I hadn't expected," he said. "I thought she wanted custody."

"Yeah," Connor concurred. "I guess some of us have hearts bigger than our dreams."

Luke slapped him on the shoulder. "Well, I'm sure you're looking at a life filled with surprises. Will you tell Mrs. Pearson that I'm heading back to the office?"

"I will."

Connor peered out into the restaurant and saw that things had quieted down somewhat, probably the lull before the lunchtime rush. He saw that Shelly had seated Mrs. Pearson, Valerie and Max in the back booth on the side opposite the windows. She called the order to Dan, placing the ticket on the order wheel before coming back toward the office.

He followed her inside and closed the door behind them.

He was ready when she turned into his arms and wept her heart out. He wept with her because he knew how she felt; the baby had been an important part of his dreams, too.

"That was the bravest thing I've ever seen," he praised, rubbing her back. "I don't know that I could have done it."

"I didn't want to!" she cried, punching a fist into his chest. "But I...just couldn't throw away *her* life to make mine the way I wanted it."

"If it's any comfort," he said, "she looked as though you've given her her life back."

"I think it'll work."

"I think so, too."

"Well." She pushed out of his arms and sniffed. "I have to get to work. Poor Betsy has run her legs off." Her eyes, concentrating on the front of his sweater, raised reluctantly to his eyes. "But we have to talk sometime."

"Tonight?" he asked.

She sighed regretfully. "I'm open late tonight."

"Valerie will have the baby," he said, "so call me when you close up and I'll come down and walk you home."

"Okay." She wrapped her arms around his neck. "I love you, Connor."

He kissed her soundly. "I love you, Shelly." He took off at a brisk pace. He had a lot to do.

Chapter Thirteen

Shelly knew Connor loved her, but was she ever going to be able to convince him now that they should be married? She couldn't imagine how.

It was early evening, a relatively quiet dinnertime that Shelly welcomed considering how busy the day had been. And with her focus split among the various crises in her life, she was grateful for the slower pace.

She sent Betsy home in the afternoon with a bonus for showing up on a moment's notice.

"That's okay," she said. "A few of us are just making plans to go backpacking in Canada next summer, so I'm happy to work anytime. Just call me."

Shelly hugged her. "I'll do that. If things go according to plan, I'll need some free time soon. I'll call you as soon as I know."

She seemed pleased with the idea.

"There's a lady crying in that back booth where I sat with Mrs. Pearson," Valerie whispered to her as she waved her ticket. "She says she's okay, but all she ordered was a chocolate milk shake. Do you mind making it? It's been a while since I've done one.''

''No, I'll take care of it. Why don't you take Max home? I'll be another couple of hours.''

''I can stay,'' Valerie insisted.

''No. Go home.''

Shelly was suddenly engulfed in a fervent embrace. ''Shelly,'' Valerie said tearfully, ''I don't know what to say about this. I'm sure there's no one else in the world who'd have done this for me. And I still can't believe you did it. Was Connor mad?''

''No. He's in complete agreement. We're both sure you're going to do just fine.''

''I will.'' Valerie hugged her even tighter. ''I'm going to be the best mother there ever was. And I'm going to work so hard for you.''

''Well, you certainly did today.'' Shelly patted her shoulder. ''Now, take your baby home. His nighttime bottle is in the fridge. And you can help yourself to whatever you want. Just move the crib into your room. Oh. And take a piece of coconut cream pie home with you. Connor loves it.''

''Okay.''

The shake ready, Shelly looked toward the back booth and saw Ruby Cade sitting in the corner, a hand shielding her eyes. She was a pretty redhead who'd come home to Jester about three years earlier after a considerable time away. She was in partnership with Honor Lassiter in The Mercantile. She was married, though her husband had some kind of job that kept him away a lot, and Shelly had seen him only twice. He'd been handsome, as she recalled, with a military bearing.

Ruby was one of the Main Street Millionaires, so Shelly guessed that whatever troubled her wasn't financial. And she had no children, so that probably left some sort of marital difficulty.

No stranger to difficulties of most kinds, Shelly delivered the milk shake and slipped into the booth opposite Ruby, determined to help.

Ruby raised tear-filled green eyes to her.

"I'm sorry," she said, snatching a napkin from the dispenser and dabbing at her nose. "I hate people who make scenes."

Shelly looked around at the only other customer in one of the front booths. "No one around to notice. Is it anything you want to talk about?"

Ruby shook her head and tore the paper end off the straw's wrapper. "Thanks, but I'm not even sure what's going on. I'm just...blue."

"That infusion of chocolate should help."

Ruby forced a smile. "Since I couldn't get it intravenously, I thought a milk shake was the next best thing."

"Everything okay at The Mercantile?"

"Yes. We have some great stuff for Valentine's Day. You'll have to come and look."

"I will," Shelly promised, then slid out of the booth. "If you ever do want to talk, I'm not a bartender, but I'm the next best thing."

Ruby drew a deep breath. "Maybe you need to talk, too?" she asked. "Honor was in at lunchtime, and said the mother of your baby turned up."

Shelly nodded, a small pain pinching in her chest. Gradually a small sense of hope was beginning to replace the pain. "Valerie just waited on you. She just needs another chance."

"Yeah." That seemed to mean something different, something significant, to Ruby. She took a deep sip of the shake. "Mmm," she said with approval. "Good stuff, Shelly. By the way, I vote for fixing the church roof first, too." She smiled wistfully. "I remember going to bingo parties there with my mother and her friends."

"Okay. I'll add your vote. Call me if you need me."

"You, too."

The restaurant was empty at closing time. Shelly locked the door and turned the Closed sign to face the glass.

Dan, for whom things had been so slow the past few hours that he'd already cleaned up, gave her a big hug before heading for the door.

"You're very special, Shelly," he said, touching her cheek with paternal benevolence. "You learned all the skills your parents had for running a good, welcoming place, but you acquired other skills they sometimes let slip in the interest of the business. I know they loved you very much, and I mean them no disrespect, but there should have been more fun in your life and less restaurant. There were times when *you* should have come first.''

He pinched her chin. ''But you're smart enough to put your family first, to give, even when it isn't convenient. To open your heart to people as well as your place. What you did for that little girl and that baby was heroic. I'm so proud of you.''

''It was just…right,'' she said, waving off the praise.

''Right is often the hardest thing to do.'' He kissed her forehead and zipped up his coat. ''And sometimes—'' he bumped his knuckle against her chin ''—you have to think hard to know what the right thing is for *you*.''

''And I suppose you know what that is for me,'' she said, walking him to the door.

He nodded. ''I'm sure you'll figure it out. You've gotten so smart lately. See you tomorrow.''

Everything ready for the following day, Shelly counted out the till, put the deposit in the safe and was about to call Connor, when he knocked on the door.

She let him in, whatever security she'd once felt in their relationship rushing out as the cold night air rushed in.

''Valerie and Max get home okay?'' she asked, pulling off her apron.

''Yes. They went to bed early.''

''Did she bring you your coconut cream pie?''

''She did.''

She'd walked into the back as they talked. She hung up her apron, reached for her coat and turned to find him right behind her.

"I saved it to share with you," he said.

"You did?" She clutched the coat to her as her heart began to race. She mustn't read too much into that. He'd said he loved her. He just didn't want to marry her. Well, she had to straighten him out on that score. "Did you know that sharing coconut pie is a betrothal ritual to the seagoing natives of Burundi?"

He took her coat from her and held it open. "There are no seagoing natives in Burundi," he said. "It's a long way from the ocean."

"Hmm." She buttoned her jacket and dug into her pocket for her hat. "*National Anthropology Magazine* has misinformed me."

In a move she didn't see coming, he snatched the hat from her, took her into his arms and kissed her until she had to wriggle free and gasp for air.

"You can shine me on about that," he said, holding her close by the collar of her coat, "but don't lie to me about this. Do you love me?"

"Yes," she answered breathlessly.

"And do you think of us as bricks held together by mortar, or as—"

"Two flowers in a vase," she supplied quickly. "I'm a rose and you're a sort of...snapdragon."

He kissed her again and she knew without understanding why he *had* just been waiting for her to be ready to marry him.

"Then..." he said when he drew away, as breathless as she was "...I'd like to hear that proposal again."

She could barely muster the air to form the words. "Will you marry me?"

"Yes," he replied. "Did you know that in the betrothal rituals of the snowbound Laplanders, though it's traditional for the woman to propose marriage, the prospective bridegroom still offers her a ring of engagement?"

"I didn't know that," she breathed. "They must be in collusion about the proposal."

"Or he carries a ring in his pocket to be prepared."

"I hadn't thought of that."

He walked her to the door. "There's a second step to that tradition."

"What's that?"

"They seal their promise to each other with gewürztraminer at the Heartbreaker."

Her eyes widened. "How did you know I like that?"

"I read it," he said, leaning close enough to kiss her again, "in *National Anthropology Magazine*. Come with me."

"Anywhere," she said as they stepped out into the cold night air. She locked the door, pocketed her keys, and he caught her hand and led her across the street to the Heartbreaker.

When he pushed the door open, she was a little surprised to see almost everyone she knew there. They each came through at some time or other, but seldom all at once.

She suddenly understood why, when they shouted, "Surprise!"

Connor drew her to the middle of the room where a large white sheet cake and plates sat, the cake bearing the words *Congratulations Shelly and Connor* in red frosting. Two large entwined hearts crowned by a diamond ring were drawn above the words.

Dev came to stand behind the table, while her friends crowded around—Dean, Finn and Henry, Jack Hartman, Amanda Bradley, Gwen Tanner and all the ladies from the boardinghouse, Luke McNeil, Ruby Cade and Honor Lassiter. The mayor was there with his wife, but there was no sign of Paula Pratt.

"Sorry about the mayor," Dev said quietly as the conversation rose to a deafening roar. "He just happened to be here." Then he clapped his hands for quiet.

"Let's have your attention," he said. "Dr. O'Rourke has invited us all here because he has something important to say. And he wants witnesses."

There was a roll of laughter, then quiet when Connor reached into the breast pocket of his jacket. He held up a sparkling round-cut diamond in a simple gold setting. "Shelly," he said with a gravity that made her focus on his eyes. "Will you marry me?"

"But I just asked *you*," she pointed out in a whisper.

"As Dev said," he whispered back, "I want witnesses."

"Yes," she replied as their friends laughed.

He took her left hand and slipped the ring on her third finger. Then he took her in his arms, dipped her sideways with theatrical flair and kissed her.

Cheers rose and shook the rafters of the Heartbreaker.

"When's the wedding?" Amanda asked as Dev began to slice and serve the cake.

"Valentine's Day," Connor replied.

Shelly hugged him tightly at that. "You certainly have all the answers," she said.

"Where you going on your honeymoon?" Nathan asked.

Shelly looked up at Connor, wondering if he had an answer to that, too.

He reached into his breast pocket again and withdrew an envelope that he handed to her. "You can answer that one," he said.

She opened the envelope, pulled out two round-trip tickets and gasped when she read their destination.

"Tuscany!"

Breathless, she opened a brochure for an Italian cooking course at Casa Ombuto included with the tickets. Pictures showed a beautiful villa, a swimming pool, students eating around a candlelit table.

"'Learn pasta to pastries,'" she read. "'Fifty kilometers south of Florence. Saturday to Saturday. Four hands-on cooking sessions, a visit to the vineyard, to a local producer of olive oil and a shopping trip.' Connor!"

She couldn't believe it. The trip she'd dreamed of.

"But," she asked worriedly, referring back to the brochure, "are you going to be one of the 'nonparticipating partners enjoying the sights and golfing?' On our honeymoon?"

"No." He wrapped his arms around her again. "I'm enrolled, too. I want you within arm's reach, even if I'm a poor student and have to be the class 'go-for.'"

"I don't think that'll happen." She laughed and hugged him. "Put the two of us together and we're cooking, even without a stove."

Epilogue

"What's happening to the church?" Barbara O'Rourke asked, pointing to the scaffolding surrounding it as she, Shelly and Max occupied the back seat of Seth Hollis's old Buick. Seth was Finn's grandson, a tall, lanky redhead who now managed to have at least one meal every day at The Brimming Cup. The attraction, Shelly knew, was Valerie, though the girl maintained she had no romantic interest in Seth, simply enjoyed talking to him. Seth, Shelly was sure, felt differently. Barbara, Connor's mother, was petite in a dark green coat over a matching dress, and a wispy hat perched atop her head at a jaunty angle. She was kind and funny and, after just two days in her company, Shelly already loved her.

"It's one of the 'Shelly Projects,'" Valerie explained from the front passenger seat next to Seth.

"Oh, I heard about those yesterday at the bookstore," Barbara said. "It's sort of Shelly's personal urban renewal."

Shelly laughed at that description. "It's just a little

financial aid to a very supportive community. I guess we can't actually roof until the spring, but in preparation, they're fixing a few other things—the chimney, the fascia boards, repairing the stained-glass window.''

After making two circuits of the block the church occupied and finding no parking place, Seth stopped in front of the church and let them off. ''I'll park in front of Shelly's and run back,'' Seth told Valerie. ''Save me a place.''

Amanda ran out to greet them in a royal-blue suit, her parka pulled on over it as protection against the cold. Snow flurried from a leaden sky. She clutched a nosegay of irises and white rosebuds in one hand.

''They're waiting for you, Mrs. O'Rourke,'' Amanda said, pointing her toward Jack, who stood in the open doorway, serving as usher.

Barbara gave Shelly a quick hug. ''I'm so happy, Shelly,'' she said. Jack waved at Shelly as he met Barbara at the bottom of the steps to escort her inside.

Valerie, too, wrapped Shelly in an embrace. ''Good luck,'' she said. ''It's going to be a wonderful wedding!'' She held Max up for Shelly's kiss.

Dressed in a snowsuit patterned like a tuxedo, Max smiled widely, showing his two perfect bottom teeth. Shelly took his little face in her hands and kissed his cheek.

''No screaming until after the ceremony, okay?'' she said.

''We'll do our best.'' Valerie reclaimed him and

shooed Shelly away. "Hurry. I hear the organ. See you after."

"You nervous?" Amanda asked, hooking an arm in Shelly's and walking her around to the side door.

"No," Shelly replied honestly. She felt wonderful. She, Connor, Valerie and Max were coexisting beautifully. The sting of having to abandon her plans to adopt Max had been replaced by satisfaction at the new happiness in Valerie, and at the anticipation of starting her own family with Connor. Valerie and Max, of course, would always be part of it.

And she was about to leave for three weeks in Tuscany. Life was about as perfect as God would allow.

"Good. Because everything's under control in the church. Mary Kay and Paula are devouring Jack with their eyes, the mayor was sort of campaigning before he went inside, trying to generate interest in some announcement he's going to make early in March, Wyla predicted you and Connor will never last, sour grapes, of course, because she stopped playing the lottery before you all became millionaires. She's been so vocal about it, whatever sympathy we might have had for her is gone. And the hospital in Pine Run paged Nathan and he had to remind them that he's serving as a best man today." She grinned at Shelly as she pulled the door open for her. "All's copacetic in Jester. Oh. And Harvey Brinkman's here, but Connor pulled him aside, and I'm not sure what he said to him, but his color still hasn't come back."

Life in a small town, Shelly thought. Why would anyone want to live anywhere else?

She walked into the dark, quiet hallway where Dan, almost unrecognizable in a suit, waited for her. He caught her hands, smiling with a pride that was almost paternal. "You're beautiful!" he said.

She'd gone back to Pine Run several days ago for a simple ivory wool suit she'd tried on her shopping trip with Connor. She'd loved its simple lines, small gold buttons and tulip neckline, but thought it impractical. It was perfect, however, for a wedding.

She'd topped it with a little ivory derby with pearls in the hatband.

"Thank you," she said, squeezing his hands. "You look handsome, too. Watch out for Mary Kay and Paula."

He smirked. "I'm a little over the hill for them."

Amanda nudged him with her shoulder. "I'm into older men. Would you promise to treat me like a queen and indulge my every whim?"

"No."

"Oh. Then, never mind."

Shelly tapped her punitively with her bouquet of white rosebuds. "Quit cruising for hunks at my wedding."

The squeak of the opening side door turned them all in that direction. Connor peered around it.

Amanda tried to close the door on him. "You're not supposed to see the bride!"

Shelly shooed her away and went to join him in the

doorway. He looked heartbreakingly handsome in a dark suit. "Something wrong?" she asked in concern.

He smiled warmly. "Not a thing. I just had to see your face. How are you?"

"Wonderful," she replied. "How are you?"

"I'm wonderful, too. No second thoughts about getting married?"

"Not one. You?"

"No. Just wanted to be sure. A lifetime's a long time."

She put a hand to his cheek. "I was just wondering if it'd be long enough."

His eyes ignited and he lowered his head to kiss her lightly. "I promise you I'll make you happy."

She brushed lipstick off his bottom lip with her thumb. "Connor, you already have. I'm already yours in my heart."

The organ music took on a suddenly louder, purposeful tone.

"I'm going," he said, as Amanda threatened to push him out the door.

Shelly peered around Amanda to keep eye contact with him. Her heart was bursting with the perfection of her life—loving Connor, seeing Valerie and Max thrive, watching small, positive changes take place in Jester while its people remained comfortingly the same. It was more than anyone deserved, but she had it, and she was running with it before anyone noticed and tried to take it away.

"See you at the altar!" she said as the door closed.

* * * * *

*Come back next month when
another Main Street Millionaire has to
catch himself a fake fiancée
in the next installment of*
MILLIONAIRE, MONTANA.
Don't miss
BIG-BUCKS BACHELOR
by Leah Vale.

*Available February 2003, only from
Harlequin American Romance.*

Coming in February 2003 from

 HARLEQUIN®

AMERICAN *Romance*®

BIG-BUCKS BACHELOR
by
Leah Vale

The latest book in the scintillating six-book series,

MILLIONAIRE, MONTANA

Welcome to Millionaire, Montana, where twelve lucky townspeople have won a multimillion-dollar jackpot. And where one millionaire in particular has just...
caught himself a fake fiancée.

MILLIONAIRE, MONTANA continues with

SURPRISE INHERITANCE
by Charlotte Douglas,
on sale March 2003.

Available at your favorite retail outlet.

HARLEQUIN®
Makes any time special ®

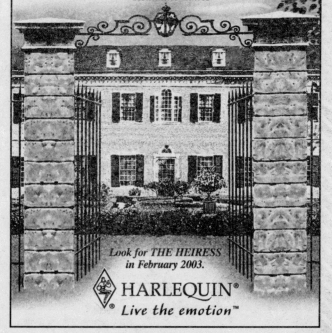

If you enjoyed what you just read,
then we've got an offer you can't resist!

Take 2 bestselling
love stories FREE!
Plus get a FREE surprise gift!

HARLEQUIN®

AMERICAN *Romance*®

Bestselling author
Muriel Jensen
kicks off

MILLIONAIRE, MONTANA

beginning in January 2003 with
JACKPOT BABY

Welcome to Millionaire, Montana, where twelve lucky
townspeople have won a multimillion-dollar jackpot.
And where one millionaire in particular has just...
found a baby on her doorstep.

The excitement continues with:

BIG-BUCKS BACHELOR by Leah Vale
on-sale February 2003

SURPRISE INHERITANCE by Charlotte Douglas
on-sale March 2003

FOUR-KARAT FIANCÉE by Sharon Swan
on-sale April 2003

PRICELESS MARRIAGE by Bonnie Gardner
on-sale May 2003

FORTUNE'S TWINS by Kara Lennox
on-sale June 2003

Available at your favorite retail outlet.

HARLEQUIN®
Makes any time special ®

Visit us at www.eHarlequin.com

HARJB